"*Your hair is like polished silver.*"

"I beg your pardon?" said Jennifer.

Duke lowered his eyes, silently cursing his audacity.

Polished silver? How poetic! Jennifer's neck arched; her hair swished against her shoulders. *Flattery?* she thought next. Her back stiffened. He was here to get a job, she reminded herself. She shouldn't be conned by pretty words. His silver tongue was far more polished than her hair.

"Regarding your application—" she began.

"I'm only looking for temporary employment."

Why did that tidbit of information send disappointment flooding through her? And why did those hot black eyes of his send tingling sensations racing up her spine?

Duke Jones might not be a threat to the law-abiding citizens of Lumberton, Jennifer decided, but he was clearly a threat to her equilibrium!

Dear Reader,

This month Silhouette **Special Edition** brings you the third (though not necessarily the last) volume of Lindsay McKenna's powerful **LOVE AND GLORY** miniseries, and we'd love to know if the *Return of a Hero* moves you as much as it did our Silhouette editors. Many of you write in requesting sequels or tie-in books—now we'd like to hear how you enjoyed our response!

Many of you also urge us to publish more books by your favorite Silhouette authors, and with this month's lively selection of novels by Jo Ann Algermissen, Carole Halston, Bevlyn Marshall, Natalie Bishop and Maggi Charles, we hope we've satisfied that craving, as well.

Each and every month our Silhouette **Special Edition** authors and editors strive to bring you the ultimate in satisfying romance reading. Although we cannot answer your every letter, we do take your comments and requests to heart. So, many thanks for your help—we hope you'll keep coming back to Silhouette **Special Edition** to savor the results!

From all the authors and editors of Silhouette **Special Edition**,

Warmest wishes,

Leslie Kazanjian, Senior Editor
Silhouette Books
300 East 42nd Street
New York, N.Y. 10017

JO ANN ALGERMISSEN
Paper Stars

Silhouette Special Edition

Published by Silhouette Books New York

America's Publisher of Contemporary Romance

SILHOUETTE BOOKS
300 East 42nd St., New York, N.Y. 10017

ISBN: 0-373-09542-2

First Silhouette Books printing August 1989

Printed in the U.S.A.

Books by Jo Ann Algermissen

Silhouette Desire

Naughty, but Nice #246
Challenge the Fates #276
Serendipity Samantha #300
Hank's Woman #318
Made in America #361
Lucky Lady #409
Butterfly #486

Silhouette Special Edition

Purple Diamonds #374
Blue Emeralds #455
Paper Stars #542

JO ANN ALGERMISSEN

believes in love, be it romantic love, sibling love, parental love or love of books. She's given and received them all. Ms. Algermissen and her husband of more than twenty years live in Florida with their two children, a weimarener and three horses. In such beautiful surroundings with such a loving family, she considers herself one lucky lady. Jo Ann Algermissen also writes under the pseudonym Anna Hudson.

NORTH DAKOTA
SOUTH DAKOTA
NEBRASKA
KANSAS
MINNESOTA
WISCONSIN
MICHIGAN
IOWA
ILLINOIS
INDIANA
MISSOURI
• Kansas City
★ Jefferson City
Lake of the Ozarks
• *Lumberton*
Springfield
KENTUCKY
OKLAHOMA
ARKANSAS
TENNESSEE
MISSISSIPPI
ALABAMA
TEXAS

Underlined places are fictitious.

Chapter One

"I suppose you think we should make a banner to welcome Duke Jones home," Sheriff "Big Jim" Elmo sneered. He raised his beefy hand, thumb and forefinger inches apart, holding his unlit cigar between the next two fingers. "Yes sirrreeee, bobtail, I can see it all now. 'Crime Wave Welcome!'"

Sophie Clarmont, the one person in the town hall's employee lounge who ever dared to disagree with the sheriff, shook her head. "We'd better start welcoming anyone who drives through Lumberton. Otherwise we're going to be a ghost town before the year 2000."

"Are you addled, Sophie? Nobody wants our little town to become a penal colony."

"Duke Jones isn't exactly a crime wave." Sophie let her bifocals slide to the end of her nose, a clear sign that she was becoming annoyed. "Our youngsters can hardly wait to turn sixteen so they can drive to Springfield or Kansas City to get a job."

"That's just my point. What's he gonna do once he gets here? Who's gonna give *Duke* a job? He's gonna have to steal to survive."

Jennifer McMann was half listening, half directing her attention to her paperback book, but at this she blurted, "There's two jobs I know of—my brother is looking for a grocery clerk and . . ."

Big Jim snorted, "Your brother isn't gonna hire him."

"And . . ." Jennifer raised her head, wishing she'd kept her mouth shut but irritated enough by Big Jim's pompous attitude to finish her sentence. After all, she *was* the mayor of this town. "And there's the job in the county maintenance department that's gone begging for months."

Jennifer stuck her nose back between the pages of her book and pretended to ignore the sheriff's guffaws to her comment. A silky curtain of blond hair fell forward to shield her heart-shaped face. One more laugh, she silently fumed, and you'll be arresting me for homicide! He couldn't arrest me, she silently corrected. He would be the victim!

Daily, Jennifer considered skipping coffee and heading straight to her office, but the morning ritual was a tradition her father had started decades ago. Raised as the only daughter of a small-town politician, she was astute enough to realize that any big changes she wanted to make in the future would be defeated if she snubbed Big Jim Elmo or the coffee klatch. That knowledge kept her from echoing the sentiments espoused by the title of the book in her hands—*Gone with the Wind*.

"Softhearted sentimentality isn't going to keep the crime rate at zero level," Big Jim said, looking directly at Sophie.

"Now, Big Jim, don't be touchy. I merely pointed out that I'd be losing this job, too, unless some of the youngsters I taught in first grade return to Lumberton." Sophie was Buffalo County's child-welfare worker.

The sheriff had been leaning his chair back; now the front legs slammed against the wooden floor. "Duke Jones is a chip off the old block. Jebediah Jones spends more time in the county clink for being drunk and disorderly than he's spent in that ramshackle hovel he calls a home."

Milly Walters choked on her sip of coffee. She was the county tax collector, but she was also the wife of the Methodist minister. She patted her prim lips with a lace-edged handkerchief, then looked down her narrow nose at the sheriff and admonished, "Shame on you, Jim Elmo. Just last Sunday my husband's sermon was about sins of the father being passed on to the child."

Raising her hand to her lips, Jennifer hid her grin. Everybody in town knew Big Jim's wife had to plant her elbow in her husband's belly to keep his snoring down to the same decibel as roaring thunder.

"I heard Reverend Walters's sermon," Big Jim blustered, slightly offended by Milly's tilting her persnickety nose toward the ceiling. "My eyes are shut so I can medidate on the minister's good words."

"And here I thought you were still checking out the backside of your eyelids for holes," Sophie gibed. "That's the excuse you gave when you were in my reading class."

"Ladies, you're sidetracking the issue. The upcoming crime wave is the real problem—a real humdinger of a problem." Big Jim wiped his mouth on his sleeve. His narrowed eyes circled the table.

Tim Farrell, Buffalo County's recorder of deeds, yawned and gave the sheriff a sleepy blink of his eyes.

Rising from his chair, Big Jim shot him a quelling glare. "My eyes are gonna be wide open while I'm cruising Main Street. Yes, sirree, bobtail. All Duke has to do is spit on the sidewalk and he'll be sharing a cell with his daddy. You women keep your doors locked at night, you hear? Especially you, Jennifer."

"Soon as I find the key," Jennifer promised, openly smiling at him. Like most of the other townsfolk in Lumberton, the keys to the Victorian house she'd inherited from her parents had been misplaced the same day her grandparents had moved the furniture inside it.

"You have me to thank for keeping law and order around here," Big Jim muttered. He hiked his britches up, then patted the holster strapped to his leg. "Nothing's gonna change just because Duke Jones rode into town on a fancy motorcycle. You can count on me to protect you."

Before Jennifer could point out that she rode a dirt bike to work and no one gave it a second thought, Big Jim strode through the door.

Sophie, Milly and Tim chorused a loud groan.

"Ladies and gentleman," Jennifer mockingly chastised, "he'll hear you."

Tim, a man who seldom spoke, nervously pushed his fingers over the sprig of hair he'd combed over his balding head. "I do seem to recall Duke Jones being arrested for stealing."

"Shoplifting. Arrested but not convicted," Sophie amended.

"Oh, dear," Milly twittered, covering her flat chest with the hand holding the hanky. "Maybe I should lock my doors. I wouldn't want anything to happen to my new television set. Who knows what sort of riff-raff Duke's been running around with in Kansas City. Why," she gasped, "Big Jim could be right. Duke could be casing Lumberton for one of those street gangs. Robbery! Rape!"

"Old scandals and septic tanks have something in common—they both stink when stirred," Sophie responded tartly. "Shoplifting isn't armed robbery. I think we can all still sleep soundly at night."

"Where there's smoke, there's fire," Milly countered primly.

"Which reminds me, I need to check the cost of a sprinkler system for city hall." Closing her book, Jennifer glanced at her wristwatch. "It's time to get to work."

Within minutes, the four of them had rinsed their coffee mugs, wiped the table and started toward their respective offices. Tim and Milly exited from the lounge, turned right and strolled down the corridor; Jennifer and Sophie turned left.

"It burns me up to hear them malign Duke," Sophie said indignantly. "He was a darling little angel in my class. Smart as a whip, too. Big Jim was a couple of years ahead of him and struggling with his vowel sounds when Duke was reading at the second-grade level. Duke had a real thirst for knowledge.''

Jennifer chewed the inside of her lip, silently praying Sophie wouldn't remember what a dummy she'd been. Big Jim was a shining star pupil compared to her. Unaware of doing it, she clutched her purse to her chest and fingered the pages of the paperback book.

"Stop fidgeting, Jennifer. It wasn't your fault you were a Roadrunner any more than it was Duke's fault that he had to drop out of high school.''

Roadrunner—what a misnomer, Jennifer thought. She remembered each group being allowed to choose its own name. The Roadrunners, Jennifer's group, had wanted to race through the preprimers but were unable to accomplish the feat. What they had lacked in reading speed, they'd made up for with originality when they'd chosen their name.

"And it wasn't your fault that your hearing loss wasn't detected in kindergarten. Back in those days, we didn't have eye and ear screenings. It's amazing what you did learn by lipreading.'' She placed her hand on Jennifer's arm. "I had faith in you. Why do you think I let you get by with memorizing everything you did hear and letting you spout it back verbatim? Your memory was phenomenal, even in first grade.''

Automatically, Jennifer touched the small hearing aid in her ear. Though small, it always felt the size of the banner Big Jim wanted strung across Main Street.

"Stop fiddling with your hearing aid," Sophie admonished kindly. "Just be thankful your problem was solved in fifth grade. Poor Duke! I imagine he has scars on his soul from trying to live down his father's reputation. Everybody expected him to be the rotten apple in the bottom of the barrel.''

"And everyone expected the mayor's daughter to be a goody-two-shoes," Jennifer said dryly.

"You both fulfilled the town's expectations. I just wish I could have done something to help Duke." Sophie grimaced, sighed, then made a schoolmarmish *tsk*ing sound. "Ah, well, I guess Big Jim must be right when he accuses me of trying to put golden halos on wicked little children's heads."

"Big Jim was lousy at math, too. He never could tell a plus from a minus. According to my calculations, your putting halos on the wicked was a definite plus for the children in Lumberton."

Sophie's hand with its tiny liver spots lightly tightened on Jennifer's arm. "Remember how I used to paste a gold star on a child's hand when they did something extra special?"

Jennifer nodded.

"The day you tossed your hat in the ring to run for mayor, I wanted to glue a whole box of stars on you. Lumberton needs your youth and vitality to get us turned around."

Feeling unworthy of Sophie's high praise, Jennifer ducked her head. She'd been in office six months and she wasn't any closer to solving the town's problems than her father had been.

"Don't shake your head at me. You're not only bright, you've got an open mind, a keen sense of fairness. I disagree with Jim about children inheriting their parents' flaws, but I do think children are often blessed with their parents' virtues. Once you get comfortable in your father's shoes, you'll have the whole town marching in the direction of prosperity."

"Marching?" Jennifer chuckled. "Considering the fact that I'm still tone-deaf, I'd say you're expecting a miracle."

Sophie chuckled as she unlocked the door of her office. "We'll see, m'dear. Who knows? You may surprise yourself."

On that note of optimism, Jennifer walked with a lighter step than usual. Maybe, she mused, she could make a difference in the final outcome of Lumberton. She had to do something or by the time the next state census was taken, the town her forefathers had founded would be removed from the map of Missouri. Right now, being the county seat of government was the life jacket keeping the town's economy afloat.

She breezed through her outer office, noting in passing that her part-time secretary was late for the third time in a week. Late is better than absent, Jennifer thought. She strode into her office straight to the window overlooking Main Street. Nothing much happened in the way of excitement on Main Street, but Jennifer could while away hours dreaming of what the town could be . . . if . . .

"If what?" she muttered. "If the government decides to launch spaceships from mid-America? If the marble in the hills around us turns to gold? If International Shoe Company reopens the factory?"

None of her fantasies were realistic. She knew it, but those unlikely happenings were preferable to reality. Lumberton was on the endangered species list. Unless something positively miraculous happened, her job, like Sophie's teaching job, would be eliminated.

You don't have two first-grade classrooms without students; you don't have a mayor without townspeople.

Jennifer jutted her pointed chin forward stubbornly, causing her blond hair to sway against her shoulders. Like her sugar-sweet disposition, the color of her hair didn't come naturally; it was acquired out of a bottle from the local beautician. The platinum color made her small features look angelic, but she knew she could be as stubborn and mean tempered as a Missouri mule in the privacy of her own home or when she gunned her dirt bike across the tracks she'd made on the trail that overlooked the lake.

Her blue eyes widened as she caught sight of Duke Jones parking his motorcycle outside her brother's grocery store. Dressed in blue jeans and a blue-striped, short-sleeve shirt, he didn't look any different than any other man on the street.

"He was there yesterday when I was there," she murmured, wondering why he was back again today.

A slow smile curved her mouth as she corrected her initial impression. He was not like any other male. Duke Jones stood out in a crowd. Her brow furrowed. Or is it that he stands apart from the crowd, she silently mused.

He'd been at the checkout counter when she'd noticed him. His meager selections had almost matched the amount of money he'd extracted from his jeans pocket. Milk, bread, hamburger, dried beans, rice, laundry detergent and a bar of soap. Oh, yes, and a peppermint stick.

Funny how she could remember what he'd bought down to the last item, but she'd been so distracted that she'd forgotten the pound of margarine she'd gone to the store to purchase.

Oh, yes, she'd noticed him. What red-blooded American woman who hadn't been on a date in six months wouldn't notice him? She was a little deaf, but she wasn't blind. Duke Jones was the best-looking male to cross the county line in years.

So she had covertly stared at him.

He wasn't handsome, not in a classic sense. His straight dark hair was cut shorter than a Greek god's. His nose might have been straight at one time, but somebody's right hook had altered the original perfection. And his body wasn't muscle-bound, like a man who spent hours lifting weights. He wasn't a giant-sized man, like Big Jim, but he wasn't a shrimp, like Tim, either. Duke was . . . just right.

Jennifer grinned at her mental assessment, but it really was the only way to describe him.

Maybe it's the way he moves, she thought—sort of graceful in a masculine way. Although his biceps didn't bulge, he did have broad shoulders and narrow hips. Of course, she'd religiously kept her eyes from straying to his buns. It wouldn't do for the female mayor of a small town to be seen ogling a man's backside.

Maybe it's his eyes, she thought. He'd barely glanced at her in the store, but those black eyes of his gave her the feeling that he knew a naughty secret and he wanted to share it with her. They had been warm, with a smidgen of laughter in them. They'd made her skin feel alive and tingling.

Her smile slipped a notch as she remembered how those dark eyes had frosted over when her brother, George, had asked Duke what the hell he was doing back in Lumberton. With the blink of an eye he'd converted the warmth into shards of ice.

She also remembered quelling the urge to take the long loaf of French bread in her hand and smack it over her brother's head. George had the tact and grace of the proverbial bull in a china shop.

The only reason he hadn't run for mayor against her was that several townspeople had made it known that they wouldn't vote for George if he was running for dogcatcher. His sign over the cash register—In God We Trust, Everybody Else Pays Cash—hadn't endeared him to the local farmers. Their father had always carried accounts for those who needed it during the long spells between planting and harvesting crops. George had taken over running the store; they sure as shootin' weren't going to let him take over running the city.

So why was Duke back at the store today?

Jennifer's wandering thoughts were brought to a screeching halt when she saw Duke slam the grocery store's door and stand with his hands on his hips in the street outside.

"Mayor!"

Startled, Jennifer's hand flew to her chest. She spun around as though she had been caught peeking in a neighbor's window.

"For heaven's sake, Clementine, don't sneak up on me. If the window had been open you'd be scraping me off the sidewalk."

Clementine giggled. "Did you see him yet?"

"Who?"

"Who! The only man in town worth looking at."

"I suppose you mean Duke Jones?"

"You suppose right. I swear, Mayor, one look at him and I almost had heatstroke! My whole body felt as though it had caught fire!"

"I wouldn't have heatstroke if I were you." She plopped down in the desk chair and thumped a bill that had a tire and crowbar insignia in the left corner. Clementine was young and impressionable, not to mention prone toward gossiping to avoid work, and Jennifer knew she had to direct Clementine's attention toward the reason for her being at city hall— work. "The ambulance is still sick. Do you think Bob over at the garage sending us our last unpaid bill is a hint that he isn't going to work on it until the city settles up its account?"

"Who cares about a silly old ambulance! I exaggerated a little about having heatstroke."

Jennifer watched Clementine's cropped curls bob as she bounced across the room. Three-inch heels should have made bouncing an impossible feat, she mused, but Clementine managed. Her Shirley Temple curls weren't the only thing bouncing, either. Her ample bosom provided a challenge for the most tightly sewn buttons to stay in place.

Pressured by the town's only attorney, Clementine's father, Jennifer had hired her on a trial basis. Being the daughter of a prominent family did have advantages.

Every morning, Jennifer considered grabbing a handful of Clementine's curly locks and giving her a good sound shake in the hope of getting her motivated. Only the certainty that Jennifer would be sued in a minute and the fact that she had to maintain the decorum befitting her job as mayor kept her hands loosely folded on her desk.

"It's springtime and I'm in love," Clementine announced dramatically, folding her arms over her jiggling breasts, rolling her eyes and sighing.

"Terrific. You're also late."

"Late, schmate! Who cares about opening mail and filing when the most gorgeous male in the world is out there waiting for me?"

"I care," Jennifer responded dryly. "Do you have the tape of yesterday's mail ready?"

Since Clementine couldn't type more than ten words a minute, with errors, they'd mutually agreed for her to tape the contents of the incoming and outgoing correspondence. Jennifer dictated her responses. Clementine's best friend, who worked for the agriculture bureau, typed from the dictation.

Jennifer readily admitted this office procedure was deplorable, but it solved both their problems. She could listen to the tapes while doing her work, and Clementine didn't have to use up the world's supply of white-out.

"It's on your desk." Clementine sighed again, this time in exasperation. "I guess I'd better get busy, huh?"

"That would be nice." Jennifer's phony smile didn't reach her eyes. "I'll be out of the office this afternoon going over this month's budget with the accountant. I'd appreciate it if you'd be here to answer the telephone."

"No problem. You know I love talking on the phone. Besides, if there's a personal emergency I can always turn on the recorder."

Jennifer stifled a loud groan. Clementine's inefficiency made her own problems twice as difficult. For a scant second, she almost wished Duke Jones would kidnap Clementine. The mental image of Clementine perched on the back of Duke's motorcycle, the two of them riding off into the sunset, had her heartily applauding in the background. Big Jim would be rid of his crime wave; she'd be rid of her lackadaisical secretary.

Poor Duke, she thought. He'd be getting the stick end of life's lollipop, again.

"I'm goin' already. You should be glad I didn't call in sick. I'm missing an absolutely fantastic sale. Designer's clothing…Neiman Marcus…Kansas City."

"Go!" Jennifer mouthed during the pauses.

"I don't know why you have to be so bossy. Dad says—"

"Close the door on your way out, please."

She could barely tolerate Clementine's twitters; she would not tolerate listening to Clementine's father's archaic, hillbilly philosophy.

"Well!" Miffed, Clementine waggled her finger in front of her boss's nose. "Before you so rudely interrupted me, I was just going to tell you that my daddy thinks that next to my mama, you're the sweetest thing around these Ozark Mountains. He insists that I work here so you and Mama can both be a good influence on me."

Jennifer continued to smile sweetly, but she felt as though her face would crack at any moment. Clementine's father would hang me from the highest oak tree in the town square if he knew the real me, Jennifer mused.

With that thought in mind, she located the tape marked with a postage stamp, inserted it into the tape recorder and put the earphones on her head. A push of the button later, she was listening to a letter of complaint regarding the sanitation department's new regulation that trash containers be placed at the curb. In the last budget cut, she'd been the one to recommend that change. Woe be unto anyone who dared to mess with a citizen's trash pickup service. Jennifer had had more complaints over this issue than when she'd had a dead elm removed from the town's square.

A "dog at large" complaint followed the trash complaint. Then, Clementine's voice alternately droned and yawned as she began reading what she considered to be the junk mail. Responses to Jennifer's query letters to various corporations about locating light-manufacturing plants near Lumberton obviously bored her.

The last two letters had Jennifer holding her breath. Both companies regretted to inform her that they weren't currently expanding their operations but that they would consider Lumberton as a future site.

She'd clicked off the recorder, removed the headset and leaned back in her swivel chair when she heard a knock.

Clementine burst through the door.

"He's here!" she whispered in awe. She giggled, fluffed her hair and checked her nylons for runs. "He wants to see you!"

Jennifer didn't have to ask who *he* was. From the rosy pink tinting of Clementine's cheeks to the sparkle in her eyes, the answer was apparent. She couldn't help but wonder why Duke Jones would be coming to her office.

And then it hit her.

It had been barely an hour since she'd made the remarks about there being only two jobs in town. One was at her brother's grocery store; the other was in the city's maintenance department. She'd seen Duke slam the doors as he left the grocery. George must have refused him a job.

Oh, Lord have mercy, she silently groaned. He's here seeking the only other job in town! She'd have Big Jim leading a lynch mob if she hired him.

"Show him in, please." Show him out, her mind amended. Or tell him I'm out! Tell him the mayor's over fixing the ambulance! Tell him I've just left on a world cruise to promote Lumberton to the Japanese and the Germans!

"He filled out an application form!" Clementine clasped her hands together. "Don't you need an assistant?"

"That's supposed to be your job," Jennifer responded dryly. She had been looking for an acceptable reason for firing Clementine, but she surely didn't want Duke Jones sitting in her outer office as Clementine's replacement.

"I could quit—" Clementine's brow puckered "—but then I wouldn't be here with him, would I?"

"Very logical conclusion, Clementine."

Clementine chewed her bottom lip, straining for another brilliant idea. "If he were mayor, then..."

"Yoo-hoo!" Jennifer crooned sweetly. "On your way back from never-never land, would you show Mr. Jones into *my* office? After you get him elected mayor, he'll be able to find his own way in here."

"Oh!" Clementine grinned an apology. She was intelligent enough to realize her boss might have taken offense at her remark. "I was just thinking out loud. No harm intended, Mayor."

"None taken."

With a final shimmy of her fanny, which must have been practice for good things to come, Clementine opened the door and sashayed through it without bothering to close it behind her.

Jennifer fought a compelling urge to look busy, or swamped, or too harried to conduct an interview.

She took a deep breath to calm her nerves. How difficult would it be to simply say, "Sorry, no jobs available"? Wasn't interviewing Duke a mere formality? Like planting a tree on Arbor Day—only this time, she feared she'd be digging a hole with her teeth instead of a shovel.

Chapter Two

Jennifer Lynn McMann stared into Duke Jones's guarded eyes.

Not the least bit intimidated by her aquamarine blue eyes, Duke Jones stared back.

Although he was clean shaven, with his hair cut to a respectable length, wearing clean but unpressed work clothes, she felt sorry for him. Sorry he'd had to come back to Lumberton. Sorry her brother hadn't hired him. Sorry a strong, able-bodied man had to drop his pride in the dust and beg for a menial job with the city. What a pity!

The longer he kept his silence, the less sorry she felt for him and the more sorry she felt for her own position. From the direct glare in his eyes, he wasn't the person in her office who needed sympathy. Most likely, he'd hate being pitied more than he hated being unemployed.

Her eyes dropped first, landing on a stack of business papers.

Protocol said she should be the one conducting the interview, but what the hell would she ask him? His family had been the subject of many a raised eyebrow, and of many a head-shaking, hushed conversation. Everybody within a hundred-mile radius knew the intimate details of the notorious Jones family.

His father, Jebediah, was a drunken, unemployed roustabout; his mother had run off when she'd gotten sick to death of living in poverty; his younger sister, Bridget, attended Lumberton High School and was considered the only normal member of the entire family.

The whole county, bar none, considered the Jones family poor white trash.

The common greeting, "Hi, how are you doin'? How's the family?" was out, she mused. Those were definitely unsuitable questions. Jennifer could be Missouri-mule stubborn, but she wouldn't make an ass out of herself.

"I understand the city has an opening in the maintenance department," Duke said in a clipped, monotone voice.

She raised her eyes.

He appeared to be focusing his eyes on the papers she'd been staring at, but she had the distinct impression that he knew the whereabouts of every ounce of air she breathed in and out of her lungs.

"Yes."

"You didn't fill the vacancy earlier this morning?" He'd heard that flimsy excuse at the grocery store.

His voice remained flat, but she could have sworn she heard a sneering quality. His face still held the same bland expression.

"No."

Once again she had the sinking feeling he was the one conducting the interview and she was the nervous applicant. She had to get control or she'd be heaping recriminations on herself for being incompetent the moment he slammed the door and departed for parts unknown.

"What are your qualifications?"

Duke leaned forward and placed his application on her desk. "It's all on there."

Jennifer's stomach sank deeper and deeper. She scanned the front page, opened it to the center pages, then flipped it to the back in a matter of seconds. His penmanship was neat, his letters perfectly formed. Sophie would have been proud of him.

She glanced up. Before he had a chance to straighten his face, she saw one eyebrow raised and his lips drawn askew. The next instant, his face resumed its former lackluster expression.

Had he guessed that she hadn't read his application? Careful, Jennifer, be very careful, she coached herself silently. Duke Jones wasn't born yesterday and he isn't impressed with your pedigree. You're going to have to earn your salary today.

She excused her cursory glance at his application by saying, "We're fairly informal here at city hall. Why don't you tell me what skills you have that make you think you're the man for the job?" Her lips stretched into a sickly smile. "What type of experience do you have?"

"The usual. Carpentry. Plumbing. Electrical. Masonry work. Some custodial work during the off-season in the construction industry."

Short, succinct and to the point, she mused, wishing she could be as concise. Right now every excuse she could think of for not hiring him entailed a fifteen-minute explanation. She suspected a polite "No, thank you" wouldn't suffice.

"You're sort of a jack-of-all-trades?"

"I didn't drift from one construction site to another, if that's what you're implying. I'd planned on learning a smattering of each trade so I'd have hands-on experience when I started my own business."

"Oh?" she said, breaking her promise to herself not to ask asinine questions. "I mean—" She stopped herself before she blurted, "That's nice." She cleared her throat to have a second to rid her mind of insipid thoughts.

"What I meant is, it sounds as though you've been expending your energies in a positive direction."

Even to her own ears she knew she sounded as phony and pompous as George.

She made another attempt, her mouth digging the hole deeper, as she said without thinking, "You've learned a lot, considering you're a high-school dropout."

His face remained unaltered, but his tan turned a few shades paler; his cheeks blushed a pale pink. "I have my graduate equivalency diploma and a transcript showing the hours I picked up at the junior college. I didn't bring them with me. I thought all this job required was experience and a strong back, not academic transcripts."

He's overqualified, Jennifer silently assessed. Any employer knew that hiring an overqualified employee would lead to having a disgruntled employee. From another corner of her mind came the beginnings of admiration. Given a fresh start in a city that guaranteed anonymity, he'd tried to make something of himself.

The question George had asked him yesterday zinged through her mind: What the hell *are* you doing in Lumberton? We'll only stunt your growth!

"I could get them and return later this afternoon," Duke offered when the silence became prolonged. He shifted uncomfortably in his wooden straight-backed chair. "I'm a hard worker who is eager to learn."

"Sophie Clarmont mentioned that this morning." She'd murmured her thought aloud before she realized it. Her face flushed with embarrassment. Nothing like telling him you've been sitting around gossiping about him, dummy!

"Miss Clarmont? My first-grade teacher?" Genuine surprise brought a small smile to Duke's lips. For the first time he looked at Jennifer, not as the mayor of Lumberton—the woman about to refuse him a job—but as another human being in this iceberg of a town. He rubbed his temple with his forefinger as he tried to place her. Blond hair, big blue eyes. From what he could see of her figure, she was a woman he should remember. "McMann. Jennifer McMann? Weren't we both in Miss Clarmont's class?"

Her face grew warmer as the hardness in his eyes momentarily subsided. He'd been slow to place her, but the dimple she saw as he grinned was worth the delay.

She nodded.

On a different note entirely, he added, "George's little sister?"

"Guilty as accused on both counts."

Duke inwardly cringed. She couldn't have chosen a worse cliché. Those had been his exact words, spoken when he was sixteen, standing in front of a hard-nosed juvenile judge, accused of shoplifting by her father.

Mayor McMann had had some heart, though, he remembered. Satisfied with scaring the hell out of him, her father had dropped the charges. The following day, Duke had left Lumberton, swearing with each step he took that ice would freeze over in hell before he'd return.

Last week, when he'd received a frantic collect call from his sister, Duke had wrestled long and hard with that vow. He didn't want to be in Lumberton, begging for a job, any more than George and Jennifer McMann wanted him here.

He ran his finger around the back of his shirt collar. Cold sweat had trickled down the back of his neck. He felt clammy. Dirty. He knew his palms were sweating, too, but there wasn't a damned thing he could do about it.

He needed a job.

Jennifer watched him take a second look at her. She wasn't conceited enough to consider herself fantastically beautiful, but she had never thought she was physically repellent. Now, watching the way Duke's lips were tugging downward, she wondered if she'd better go take another look to make certain. Duke

Jones was staring at her the way he would at a bug in a box—and the bug wasn't particularly attractive.

"You don't look much like George," he finally commented.

"No, I don't. He takes after the Sanders side of the family. I'm pure McMann. We're both blondes, but—" Jennifer stopped midsentence. She'd replaced her inane questions with blabbing idiotic family comparisons. At the rate she was going, she'd be asking him if he wanted to compare baby pictures unless she zipped up her mouth.

"His hair is dark blond. Yours is like polished silver."

"I beg your pardon?"

Duke dropped his eyes, silently cursing his audacity.

"Your hair. It's very pale." Silently he added, okay, lady, you've done your civic duty. You made me sweat! Why don't you just politely say, "Kiss off," so I can get the hell out of here.

Unlike Jennifer, George had enjoyed refusing him a job. In no uncertain terms, George had loftily informed him that the grocery store had a strict policy against hiring thieves. Duke had wanted to belt him in the mouth. Then, while George picked himself out of the produce section, Duke would have asked him if the same policy restricted the hiring of bullies. From what he remembered of the older man, George had always been the biggest bully in Lumberton.

Polished silver? How poetic! Jennifer's neck arched; her hair swished against her shoulders. Of course, it was only flattery. Her back stiffened. A memory of Duke Jones being very popular with the older high-school girls robbed her of the pleasure of his unexpected compliment.

He's here to get a job, she thought firmly. Don't be conned with pretty words. His silver tongue is far more polished than your hair.

"Regarding your application—"

"My sister is graduating in June. I'm only looking for temporary employment."

Jennifer's eyes blinked. Why did that tidbit of information send a rush of disappointment flooding through her? She wanted him out of town, didn't she? More specifically, she wanted him out of her office, out of her presence, out of city hall. She disliked the tingling sensations racing up her spine caused by those hot black eyes of his.

Duke Jones might not be a threat to the law-abiding citizens of Lumberton, but he was a threat to her equilibrium!

"Temporary help?" she asked, leaning back in her swivel chair. He'd given her an excuse; she would gladly take it. "The ad in the weekly paper clearly stated full-time employee."

His patience snapped. In one swift move, he was on his feet and to the door before his chair stopped teetering on its back legs.

"I've never held your brother in high esteem, but at least with him a man knows where he stands. But you did mention that you're different from him, didn't you? Yeah, lady, you're different—you'd rather pussyfoot around and be polite. Why don't you just thank me politely for inquiring about the position and toss my application in the round file." He pointed toward the waste can.

"That's enough, Mr. Jones."

"Enough? No, *ma'am*, it isn't nearly enough for what you're putting me through. Why are you bothering to be sticky sweet? Do you want me to leave here thinking how kind and gracious the mayor is? Don't worry that pretty little blond head of yours. Should I be around come November for elections, which I seriously doubt, you'll get my vote. Hell, lady, you don't need my vote! You don't have to worry about losing your job. You're a McMann! The election officials will probably let me vote three times if I cast my ballot for a McMann."

His hand was already on the brass doorknob when Jennifer blurted, "Sit down, Mr. Jones."

She should have let him go, but the truth in his accusations pricked her conscience. She was a Mc-Mann, the great-granddaughter of one of Lumberton's founding fathers. She was sitting behind the mayor's desk because of *who* she was rather than *what* her qualifications were; in fact, in one way her qualifications were completely inadequate. And even worse, she despised the thought of Duke's leaving her office thinking she was as narrow-minded as the rest of the town, prejudiced against him because he was Jebediah Jones's son, unsympathetic to the unemployment problems of a man who'd returned to his hometown.

She'd promised the voters she would create new jobs, to bring their sons and daughters back home. Nothing had been said about picking and choosing which son or daughter would be acceptable for employment. She couldn't go back on her word.

Duke Jones's applying for a job tested her mettle. Was she like George? An imperious, insensitive, hard-hearted bigot? No, by God, she wasn't! This was one test she wouldn't fail. She'd pass this test with flying colors!

"The job entails a variety of work," she said slowly. "You're qualified to do most of it—everything from fixing leaky faucets to repairing potholes in the streets."

Duke stood there feeling stunned. He watched her lips move, but what she said didn't register in his mind. She wouldn't offer him the job; he'd known that the minute he'd slammed the door on her brother's grocery store and turned toward city hall.

"Minimum wage, to start with," she continued. "That's not much considering your qualifications, but the city is on a tight budget."

"Are you offering *Duke Jones* a job?"

He couldn't quite believe his ears. To make certain she understood the upcoming consequences of such a decision, he purposely let his eyes trail over the ivory blouse beneath her navy blue suit until they fastened on the faint show of cleavage exposed. He gave her the heated look that others would attribute to her reason for hiring him.

Jennifer willed the hot blood storming from her heart to her scalp not to turn her face beet red. "Yes."

His arrogant appraisal of her physical attributes halted as though he'd come to the only red stoplight in Lumberton. His black eyes jumped to her blue eyes. He fully expected to see the same look of disdain in her eyes that he'd seen as a child on the cafeteria worker's face when she'd punched his free lunch ticket.

It took considerable effort for him to quietly ask, "Pity? Are you offering me this job because you feel sorry for me?"

Her mouth had formed a negative reply; her keen sense of honesty wouldn't let it skitter across her dry tongue. "You're qualified. Overqualified would be more accurate." *Something I certainly am not,* her conscience nagged. "You're the best man who's applied for the job."

He raised his brows, silently asking, "The only man?" He knew better than to inspect the teeth of a gift horse, but he didn't want this job to be a glorified form of welfare.

"I'll *earn* every penny the city pays me."

Jennifer heard the word he'd stressed, and she nodded. "I'll count on it. Report to Sam Wilson by eight tomorrow morning. His office—"

"Is on the terrace level." A slow smile creased his lips; only the pretentious members of the community referred to the basement offices as being on the terrace level. Heady relief surged through him. "I'll be there. Early."

Jennifer stood, then rounded her desk and crossed the worn carpet that covered the scuffed hardwood floor beneath it. Each light step caused the boards to squeak, drawing attention to her slender legs. She strove to keep her expression blank, businesslike. The closer she came to him, the harder the task grew. She wanted to smile like a sappy schoolgirl who'd impressed the captain of the football team.

"I'll check into getting benefits for you, but being a temporary employee, don't hold your breath." *Why not? You are,* she silently scolded herself. "Turn your hours in on Wednesday and you'll be paid Friday. Do you need an advance on your salary?''

"No."

Just getting a job would put an end to tapping his cash reserve. Necessity had taught him to be frugal. He'd pinch pennies for the rest of the week and then his healthy savings account would remain untouched. The money he'd saved over the years was earmarked for his own business.

The skeptical look Jennifer gave him made him shake his head vehemently. "No, thank you."

"Clementine has the employment forms you'll need to fill out before you leave."

She reached for the doorknob.

He reached for it.

Their hands touched, withdrew, then touched again. An electrical current of awareness ricocheted through both of them.

He could smell the light flowery perfume she wore; she smelled his woodsy after-shave.

He felt the softness of her skin through two layers of fabric as her arm brushed against his; she felt the heat of his breath on her scalp.

She glanced up through her lashes at him; unexpectedly, his eyes met hers. Both pairs of eyes dropped to the doorknob.

"Excuse me."

"Sorry."

Who said what wasn't clear to either of them. Blood pounded in Duke's ears; Jennifer's heart seemed to have jumped up into her throat, where it was beating like a big, bass drum.

She stepped back to let him open the door for her. The way her knees were shaking, it was a major accomplishment.

He grasped the knob as though it were a slender lifeline to sanity and swung the door open.

"After you." His voice was calm, despite his internal turmoil.

Clementine was off her tush and on her feet so fast that Jennifer thought someone else who looked like her secretary had replaced her. "Didja—" Her eyes rounded in surprise as they bounced from one face to the other. She gasped, "Oh, my God—you did hire him!"

Duke gave a low masculine chuckle. Jennifer chafed her wrist to get her blood flowing normally, then folded her arms below her chest to stop her heart from sinking to her toes. The astonishment Clementine showed would be the general reaction of the townspeople once the word was out, with one difference: Clementine would be the only one reacting with joy.

You made your decision, her conscience silently goaded. You can't be a wishy-washy female and change your mind. Stick by your guns. You're going to need them!

"You'll need to take care of the paperwork," Jennifer instructed briskly. With a weak smile, she excused herself with a curt nod and backed into her office, shutting the connecting door.

Clementine's words repeated themselves in her mind. Oh my God! You did hire him!

Nerves on edge, she began pacing between the door and the window. Her confidence in having hired the best man for the job waned with each creaky step she took. The whole town would be signing petitions to have her recalled from office.

"You can't be recalled for making the right decision," she encouraged herself, speaking out loud in her agitation.

Who are you to decide what's right and wrong? her insecurities nagged.

The mayor! No one questioned my father's decisions.

You aren't your father. He was a man, with the age and wisdom to be respected for making difficult decisions.

But Duke can do the job.

He's overqualified.

So?

He'd be discontented. He'll stir up trouble.

Dammit! That's a supposition. Stick to the facts. A man came in and applied for a job that he was qualified to do. You, being an efficient city administrator, hired him.

And now, after you clean off the tar and feathers from being run out of town on a rail, you're going to be the one seeking employment. You blew it, Jennifer. Admit it. Every pair of eyes in town is going to be watching you...and you can't afford that kind of scrutiny!

The ringing telephone pierced through her silent monologue. She waited a moment to see if her secretary would answer it.

"Get that, would you?" Clementine called from the outer office.

"Got it!" She should have known better than to expect Clementine to do two things at once. Jennifer lifted the receiver. "Mayor's office."

"Jennifer? How come you're answering the telephone?"

Recognizing her brother's voice, she wondered if there was a direct pipeline between her office and the grocery store.

"Clementine's busy."

"What happened? Did the phone ring while her nails were still wet?"

Jennifer winced. She might think unkind thoughts about Clementine's work habits, but George enjoyed picking on people.

He laughed at his own humor, then said, "I just thought I'd give you a ring and warn you."

"About what?" She clenched her teeth, hating herself for playing dumb. She knew damned good and well who, not what, he wanted to warn her about.

"Who, sister, dear. Who."

Her shoulders straightened. She was too old to play guessing games with her brother, especially when she knew the answers. "Duke Jones?"

"Yeah. He came slinking in here with his hat in his hand looking for a job. Can you imagine?"

It would take all her vivid imagination to conjure up that distorted picture. From what she'd seen of Duke, he wasn't the type of man who'd slink or beg.

"He's in my outer office," Jennifer replied sweetly. "I hired him to work in the maintenance department."

"You what!" George blasted her. "That has to be the dumbest stunt you've ever pulled. Have you lost your ever-lovin' mind?"

The hairs on the back of her neck bristled. "Not yet."

"Well, you can just un-hire him. He's a bum!"

"Bums become upstanding citizens when they're given the right job."

"I will say this for you, you gave him the right job—sweeping streets."

While George busted a gut laughing, Jennifer mentally made a note to call Sam regarding Duke's responsibilities. If necessary, she'd sweep the streets. George wouldn't have the satisfaction of spitting on the sidewalk in front of the broom Duke pushed.

She considering putting two fingers under her tongue and letting loose with a shrill whistle to stop the ugly sound of her brother's laughter. She controlled that impulse and crooned, "Was there anything else bothering you, George?"

"You're gonna have hell to pay over this."

"I'll have Clementine make out a voucher."

"Very funny, little sister—ha, ha. Everybody in town is going to wish I had run against you when they hear this piece of news."

"Maybe."

"There's no maybe about it. Only a woman would hire Duke Jones."

His insinuation was as clear as graffiti on a bathroom wall.

"You have the right as a citizen of Lumberton to question my decision but not my integrity." Her voice lowered to a pitch she felt certain he'd recognize.

Once, she'd used it when he had her so frustrated that she'd come after him with a baseball bat. "Back off, big brother. You only get one vote, same as Duke Jones."

Even over the telephone wires, she could hear George grinding his teeth. Seldom did anyone have the unmitigated gall to stand up to her brother. He didn't like it.

"Turn up your hearing aid, sis, or you'll regret not listening to me," he warned. "You're my sister, a McMann! McManns are born with enough good sense not to want to have their good name besmirched by associating it with the Joneses. You know I wouldn't be telling you this if I didn't love you."

Love me a little less loudly, would you? Jennifer said silently.

"I've only got your best interest at heart. This is our town. *We* have a leadership responsibility. You can't..."

When George climbed up on the family's soap box and started to lecture, he expected an attentive audience. Jennifer did the one thing she knew would drive George totally bonkers. Very quietly, she whispered, "Goodbye, George," and hung up the telephone.

It was foolish to cross George, but she actually felt better knowing he violently opposed her decision. He couldn't tell right from wrong any more than he'd been able to tell right from left when he'd been a child.

Jennifer cocked her ear toward the outer office. No sounds could be heard. Clementine must be playing lady bountiful and escorting Duke downstairs, she deduced, grinning.

She pulled open the bottom drawer to get her purse. George would hightail it over to city hall once he realized she was no longer listening to his sage advice. By the time he arrived, she wanted to be long gone . . . or at least out of shouting distance.

It would also be a good time to be unavailable for other irate phone calls, she thought, crossing to Clementine's desk and switching on the recorder.

Let 'em call. She planned on doing exactly what any politician who was worth his salt knew to do when the going got tough—vanish. Simply vanish.

Chapter Three

Jennifer skipped pebbles on the calm surface at the lake's edge. Although she considered this stretch of the lake her private sanctuary, she wasn't finding the peace of mind she'd sought.

What if, God forbid, George and Big Jim were right? Handing the keys to the city over to a man who had shot out every streetlight on Main Street with a BB gun when he was twelve wasn't a politically wise decision.

Plunk. The rock she'd sidearm pitched didn't make the first hop.

Skip the politics, she mused, stooping to select a flatter rock. What rankled her most was her brother's accusation that only a woman would hire Duke Jones. It galled her to admit it, even to herself, but there could be a tiny element of truth in George's statement.

Duke Jones did radiate a certain raw sexuality, drawing unsuspecting women toward his rugged good looks. Any red-blooded American woman would give Duke a second look if she passed him on the streets.

Charisma, Jennifer mused. The same sort of appeal that makes women stay up late watching old pirate movies on television. Duke exuded a special brand of swashbuckling male charisma most men sadly lacked.

From a crouched position she tossed another rock. *Plop.*

She grimaced. "Physical attraction did not motivate my decision to hire Duke Jones!"

She said it aloud, fervently, hoping to convince herself that what she'd said was true. Why lie to herself? There were other reasons she'd hired him.

Yeah, like being a sucker for the underdog. Hell, she'd been the underdog! Just because no one else shared her shameful secret didn't mean it didn't exist.

Automatically, her fingers touched her hearing aid, then brushed her hair off her shoulders. Aware of what she'd done and how most people interpreted the gesture as a feminine ploy to draw attention to her sunstreaked hair, she shook her head.

Little do they know, she mused, with a tight grimace that thinned her lips into a straight line.

Knees bent, she sat down and propped her head on her arms. Her efforts to glean at least the small satisfaction of watching a rock skip four or five times across the water's surface weren't successful. Mother

Nature's think tank hadn't provided her with the justifications she needed for hiring Duke.

So, what's the worst they're gonna say?

You're softhearted, an easy mark for a con artist. Somebody tells you a sad story and you open up the city's coffers. The mayor used city funds to purchase a few words of meaningless flattery from Duke Jones.

"Fiscal irresponsibility," she muttered.

The townspeople would make those charges, but *she* knew they were untrue. The people who'd call her softhearted were the same people who howled about her cutting the budget to the bone—the same people who complained about having to tote their trash to the street curb!

And Duke hadn't moaned and groaned. He hadn't tried to win her sympathy by telling her his sad story.

Why? Pride? From Jebediah Jones's son? Maybe, but from what little she did remember, family pride in the Jones name wasn't something handed down to Duke from his parents.

Jebediah had traded his pride for a bottle of Wild Turkey long ago. And all Jennifer could remember of Duke's mother was that she had run out on her family. If it was pride that kept Duke from relating a sad story, he certainly hadn't inherited that from his parents!

She wondered if Jebediah Jones had a glib tongue. His son had certainly flattered her. Jennifer's lower lip shot out as she blew her bangs off her forehead. "Polished silver?" she murmured.

His lyrical compliment had come unexpectedly. Frankly, she didn't think Duke had made it intentionally. He certainly hadn't repeated it; he'd changed his poetic description of her hair to "very pale." Cleverness on his part, she wondered, or an attempt to hide something soft inside him behind a tough exterior?

She made a wry face.

The voters would laugh her out of office if she tried to convince them that Duke Jones was like a black walnut: hard as rock on the outside but with a sweet treat inside. Duke Jones sweet? She'd be the one they would call nuts!

She raised her head from her arms as she heard a noise coming from around the bend. She lightly tapped her hearing aid. It sounded like a boulder falling in the lake somewhere farther around the point.

She glanced over her shoulder at the gray wall of limestone cliffs soaring a hundred feet into the sky. There were no telltale signs of a rock slide: no other boulders ripping loose from the sheer wall, no pebbles tumbling into the lake.

Slowly, she rose to her feet.

The only people who came to this secluded part of the lake were the occasional fishermen in a boat. She hadn't heard an engine or voices.

Must have been a rock, she decided, still definitely curious about the sounds she continued hearing.

Rock hopping, she wove around and across the boulders until she reached the other side of the point. She lifted her eyes from the tricky footing when she heard an earsplitting *"Whhhhoooooeee!"*

A dark head bobbed under the lake's surface, then reappeared several yards farther out from shore.

Jennifer's eyes rounded; goose bumps sprinkled across her forearms. In early spring, the water had to be freezing cold.

The swimmer sliced through the water heading back to shore.

What he lacks in brains he makes up with brawn, she mused, appreciative of his powerful breaststroke. She stood there, hands on her hips, legs spread for balance, mesmerized until he reached waist-deep water.

Her glance rose from the man's darkly furred chest to his tanned face. Duke Jones! She murmured a mild expletive. The last person she wanted to invade her private sanctuary was the cause of her problem!

Duke scrubbed the water from his eyes with his knuckles. Damn, the lake was one helluva lot colder than he remembered. But he felt good—no, better than good. He felt terrific. He'd achieved the impossible; he'd gotten a job in Lumberton!

Gingerly moving his feet across the rocky bottom, he could hardly wait to stretch out on a rock and let the sunshine warm his skin. Tomorrow, he'd be working; today he planned on whiling away the hours reacquainting himself with his old stomping ground. He'd pick Bridget up after school, take her to the local burger doodle and then they'd . . .

He felt the presence of someone before he lowered his hands from his eyes. He looked up to see Jennifer McMann standing on a rock, like a fair-haired goddess assigned to protect his watery haven from intruders.

Instantly he stopped, looking down through the crystal clear water. Great! Just great! Isn't that my kind of luck? She hires me and gives me a citation for skinny-dipping—all within a couple of hours.

"What are you doing here? Swimming?"

Duke grinned, biting back a teasing remark about her asking and answering her own question. "Freezing."

"So? What are you waiting for? Get out of the water!"

But as soon as Jennifer made this suggestion, she looked toward the bank. A pile of clothes were there. She'd been raised with a brother. White briefs were easily recognizable from this distance. She immediately grasped the problem.

"You're naked!" she gasped.

Duke glanced down as though totally shocked. In mock horror he shouted, "Oh, my God! Somebody must have ripped the clothes right off my body without me noticing! They got everything but my birthday suit!"

"Very funny, Mr. Jones. Ha. Ha." Jennifer struggled to keep the prim expression on her face; she wasn't going to let him know she thought his antics were amusing.

She turned her back on him and faced the limestone cliffs. While she silently cursed his brazenness for daring to swim in her sanctuary without a stitch of clothing on, she also wished she'd had the same amount of nerve. It wasn't that she hadn't thought of doing it. She had, on numerous occasions. But she'd always been afraid she'd get stranded away from shore, with a boat full of city officials between her and her clothes.

"Okay," Duke drawled. "You can turn around now. I'm decent."

Jennifer spun around, ready to read him the riot act until she took one look at him. Her mouth went stone dry. He was unquestionably the most handsome specimen this town had ever produced!

Drops of water glistened in his hair, reminding her of a magazine ad she'd recently seen, captioned Diamonds on Black Velvet. Those diamondlike droplets slowly dribbled down the side of his bronze-toned skin until they fell from his strong jawline to the supple smoothness of his shoulders.

He was still naked to the waist, and far more powerfully built than she'd realized.

She swallowed the tongue-lashing she'd planned on giving him. He belonged to this beautiful natural setting more than she did. She jumped off the rock where she'd been standing and turned back to her side of the point.

"Hey!" Duke shouted. "I said I was decently attired. Where are you going?"

Surprised by her immediate retreat, he'd blurted the question before thinking. Maybe he'd offended her by telling her he was decent before he'd fully clothed himself. What the hell did he know about a woman's sensibilities? He'd been too busy chasing the almighty dollar to be diverted by feminine companionship.

"Home!"

Duke hastily shrugged his arms into his shirtsleeves. The blue chambray cloth clung to his wet skin. He glanced at his sneakers. She'd be long gone before he got them on, he decided. Grabbing them in one hand, he hotfooted it in her direction.

She was out of sight when he called again. "Wait a minute!"

"What for?"

"To give me a chance to thank you." Intent on watching which way she was going, he stubbed his toe. "Ow!" His muttered street language wasn't mild as he grabbed his foot to inspect it.

Jennifer shot a longing glance toward the rock where she'd been sitting before her privacy had been so rudely interrupted, then sighed. She didn't need his thanks. She'd just been doing her job. Her eyes swung to the wooded trail that led to where she'd leaned her dirt bike against a cottonwood tree.

She knew better, but something unexplainable, something deep inside her, made her want to linger, to find out more about the man with a rough exterior and soft insides. She'd never known anyone like Duke Jones. But she couldn't stay; the last thing she needed was for anyone from town to find the two of them together here.

"Could you wait just a second?" Duke called. "I've bashed my damned toe!"

"You what?" Jennifer wheeled around and saw him hobbling toward her. Her eyes widened at the sight of blood dripping from his big toe. "How in the world did you manage to do that?"

Now that she'd stopped, Duke found himself tongue-tied. He noticed that she'd changed from her dress-for-success navy blue suit and pristine white blouse into faded jeans, a V-necked shirt and a fuzzy yellow cardigan sweater, the kind of sweater that beckoned, "Touch me and see if I'm as soft as I look!"

With an awkward gait, he closed the gap between them. "Pure clumsiness. I must not've been watching where I was going."

"I'll bet that rarely happens," Jennifer chided, more concerned about his big toe than governing her mouth. She dropped to one knee to get a better look. It looked awful. The nail was turning a purplish black. "Looks like you dropped a king-sized rock on it rather than stubbed it."

Fascinated by the way her silky hair parted when she bent over to assess the damage, he barely heard what she'd said until it registered that she was doubting what he'd told her.

"Do you think I'd purposely smash my toe to get a word with you?"

Jennifer's head jerked upward. Cast in that light, her innocent remark, one she'd intended to contain a bit of humor, sounded the height of conceit. His unfair interpretation sparked her temper.

"Are you calling me stuck-up?"

She'd called him a liar because of his reputation. What the hell! What about her reputation? According to the kids he'd hung around with, Miss Fancy Pants McMann had a frostbitten nose from having it stuck so high in the air! He shifted his weight to an old, familiar stance of defiance, to the wrong foot. He clenched his teeth with the pain and forgot to watch his words. "Yes."

Audibly gasping, she rocked back on her heels and gave him a drop-dead glare. She wasn't stuck-up and never had been. Shy, maybe. Wary, certainly. But never, never, had she been snooty to her classmates. He was as wrong about her as . . . as she'd been about him? Through her red haze of anger she watched his expression change from anger to abject contriteness.

"I'm sorry," she mumbled. "I know you wouldn't bloody your toe just to get my attention."

Apologies had been a scarce commodity in Duke's life in Lumberton. He'd seldom heard one and seldom given one. But the momentary flash of pain he'd seen in her eyes made apologizing as essential to him as breathing ... and as natural.

"Me, too. I mean it, Jennifer. I am sorry. I should be down on my knees kissing your feet for hiring me."

The irony of the situation brought a grudging smile to Jennifer's lips. She was still on her knees; all she had to do was bend forward and she could plant a big smackeroo on his injured foot. Kiss it and make it all better, she mused, remembering her mother's cure for her childhood bumps and scrapes.

Duke dropped down beside her, partially to get the weight off his foot and partially to get closer to the warmth illuminating her face. Whatever her thoughts were, they weren't bad ones of him.

"What are you thinking?" he asked quietly.

She scrunched up her nose and shook her head. "Nothing."

"Nothing?" He grinned. "Something must've tickled your funny bone. Tell me." He noticed she'd looked him hard in the face, blushed, then bent on all fours to tend to his foot. "C'mon, Jennifer. You can tell me. We've known each other forever."

Tell him that when he grins he's got the cutest, most enticing dimple that you've ever seen? Like hell. She didn't want to admit that to herself, much less say it out loud. Duke Jones is off limits, she sternly reminded herself. She'd make certain his toe wasn't broken and then she'd be on her way—without wistfully looking over her shoulder, either.

With that pep talk in mind, she said, "Can you wiggle it?"

Her perfectly rounded bottom swayed in front of his eyes as she crouched beside his leg. Mind reader, Duke thought, but answered, "Yeah."

He closed his eyes hoping to bank his wayward thoughts. The flowery fragrance she wore teased his senses. His imagination took him to mysterious forbidden places, a place where both of them were strangers meeting by a secluded lagoon, a place where he could rest his hand on the womanly flare of her hip and deeply inhale her fragrance until he could identify the mysterious woman anywhere.

He squeezed his lids shut until black spots swam before him. His hands clenched around loose pebbles as he prayed for a sharp edge to blunt the stirring of his flesh.

Jennifer glanced over her shoulder. It must hurt worse than she'd thought. He had an absolutely agonized expression on his face. Uncertain of what to do, she decided to stanch the trickle of blood. With what? Neither of them had a first-aid kit.

She pulled the tail of her shirt from her jeans and ripped it off.

Duke's eyes sprang open. His thoughts had digressed to a story in a men's magazine where the macho hero had ripped the heroine's bodice from her breasts.

"What the hell are you doing?" he muttered between clenched teeth.

Jennifer dangled the strip of red cloth in his face. "I'm gonna wrap up your big toe."

"Don't."

One touch of her hands and he'd explode. Lord have mercy on a poor sinner, he silently beseeched. He hadn't prayed in years, not since his mother had deserted him and his prayers had gone unanswered.

"Why?"

He couldn't think of a reason he could decently use. "Air," he said desperately. "A wound heals faster when fresh air can circulate around it."

One of her hands gently touched the underside of his foot as she prepared to bind the wound with her free hand.

"You're sure? I'll have to get you back up that trail. Won't it get dirty? Get infected?"

The damage had been done. She'd touched him. Fortunately, his body had been mature enough not to disgrace him, but all she had to do was notice how tight the fit of his jeans had become and the concern he saw on her face would change to disgust. Damn, there were certain parts of a man's body that were beyond control, no matter how hard a man tried to be circumspect.

He bent at the waist and pretended to examine his foot.

"It'll be all right."

"You'll have to keep it straight up."

"No problem."

"I think you ought to let me take care of it. I know you're in pain, but . . ."

"Jennifer, please . . ." He swiped the dots of perspiration on his upper lip with his shirtsleeve.

Stubborn cuss, Jennifer silently berated him. He bites his lips to keep from moaning and groaning like a kid, and when he's offered help he gets macho fever and refuses it!

She knew how to get to him. The most important thing in the world to him was his new job. "You're making it sound as though I'm making a big deal over nothing. I'm only looking after my investment."

Distracted by how what she'd said matched the dialogue in the story he'd read, he was totally baffled by her switch in tactics. The first thing he was going to do when he got back to his apartment in Kansas City would be to shred that damned magazine into tiny pieces!

"What?"

"I hired you. You won't be able to work if your foot gets infected."

"Obstinate female," he muttered, glad she was too naive to realize what she was doing to him. "Go on, Nurse Jenny."

"I'll be gentle. I promise."

That's my line, he thought. His lips twitched.

"Am I hurting you?"

He chuckled aloud. "No."

"It'll be over with in just a flash."

No hero ever said that to a heroine, he mused, his chest rumbling with contained laughter. It was a good thing she thought he was in the wild grip of pain. Never in a million years would he be able to tell her what he'd been thinking without getting his face slapped silly.

"There! All done."

Jennifer studied her handiwork for a second. The red bandage was a mite bulky, but it would do nicely. She shifted back on her heels and looked at Duke. His wicked black eyes danced with mirth. Was he silently making fun of her bandage? Granted, three snug wraps and a double knot would never make it into the medical journals, but under the circumstances she thought she'd done a damned fine job.

"What do you think?" she finally asked when he swallowed several times but hadn't made a comment.

"Great. Just great!"

"Well, I don't have much first-aid experience...." His eyes grew brighter. If she didn't know better, she could have sworn he was holding his ribs and repeatedly swallowing to keep from laughing in her face. "What is going on in that mind of yours?"

Duke leaned back on his elbows and let out a loud hoot of laughter. "You wouldn't tell me what you were thinking when I asked. I'm sure as hell not revealing my private thoughts. Fair's fair."

His laughter was infectious. She couldn't remember him laughing when they were children, except on the few occasions when he'd pulled a delightfully naughty prank to entertain the whole class. She knew she had a sappy grin on her face, but she didn't care.

"Someday," she threatened without rancor, "I'm gonna make you tell me." She straightened her shoulders and tilted her nose sky-high. In a snooty voice, she said, "After all, I am the mayor."

That sobering claim brought Duke back to reality. She was the mayor. His boss. With the capacity to fire as well as hire.

"I think I'd better be heading toward the high school," he said, getting to his feet. "My sister had a major attack of spring fever this morning and wanted to play hooky from school. I cured it by promising her a ride home on my motorcycle."

"Hey!" Jennifer dropped her pose and scrambled to her feet. Intent on rectifying any mistaken idea he had that she was serious, she missed seeing the hand he'd extended to help her up. "I was only kidding. Being mayor doesn't entitle me to be privy to your innermost secrets."

Duke wiped his palm on his jeans. Slightly affronted by her refusal to casually take a helping hand from him, he said, "I'll remember that. See you, boss lady."

For an injured man, he sure hobbles fast, she thought as she watched him eat up the uneven ground with long strides. Evidently he must have parked his bike at the top of the steeper of the two trails that led to the lakeshore. He'd have trouble jumping from rock to rock. An offer to give him a ride clung to the tip of her tongue.

Duke concentrated on focusing his eyes on the rough ground; his mind lingered on Jennifer. He was close to the rise of the point when he remembered his manners. Turning, he yelled, "Jenny!"

"Yeah?"

Her heartbeat accelerated. Maybe he'd changed his mind and decided to walk up her trail. It would be the easier path for him.

"Thanks." He pointed to the red bandage on his toe. He wondered what she'd say if he had the nerve to ask her for a date. A date with Jennifer McMann?

George McMann's only sister? Mayor of Lumberton? She wouldn't go out with Jebediah Jones's son. She'd double up with laughter if she knew he'd even had the guts to ask. And yet, from the look of anticipation on her face... No, don't mistake kindness for friendship. She's just being polite. "And thanks for the job, too."

With a flash of a dimple and a quick wave he disappeared around the point.

"You're welcome," she muttered.

What'd you expect? A ride around the square on his motorcycle? He's been living in the big city. He wouldn't be interested in a small-town hick. And what if he did want to show his gratitude by asking you out? You'd have to refuse him. To be seen with him now would give credence to her brother's claim.

She hadn't hired Duke because he was good-looking. She'd hired him because he was qualified.

"Just keep telling yourself that," she muttered, unconvinced.

Slowly, she picked her way up the trail. A quarter of the way to the top, she paused. Right there in front of her eyes was the perfect skipping rock, thin, flat and almost round. She bent down, picked it up and ran her thumb over the smooth surface.

A good skipping rock is like a four-leaf clover—a good omen—she mused, smiling as she stuck it into her jeans pocket. She'd be needing all the good luck she could garner to face the flak she would get back at city hall.

Chapter Four

Duke parked his Harley near the teachers' assigned parking spaces at the high school. The scent of dogwood and red-bud blooms should have erased Jennifer's fragrance from his mind. He hadn't touched her; her scent shouldn't be clinging to him, and yet he'd been analyzing her soft, clean fragrance since he'd left his hideaway.

There was a certain simplicity about her that intrigued him. Charm? Yeah, she'd charmed him. Who'd have thought Miss Priss of the Class of '81 would rip her clothing and grovel in the dirt to bandage his foot! Kindness? Yeah, that, too. But, all too quickly, she'd reminded him of who she was—the mayor. Consequently, he'd been put in his place, too.

Duke Jones, former hellion, general roustabout, jack-of-all-trades and master of none.

He still wondered why she'd hired him. Hell, he'd been on the brink of telling her to take her job and shove it when she'd stopped him. It might not be regarded as much here in Lumberton, but he did have his pride. If need be, he'd decided to insist on Bridget returning to K.C. with him and graduating from school there.

A bell rang shrilly.

He glanced at the school building and frowned. The high-school building had been the scene of both agonizing experiences and brief moments of ecstacy for Bridget. Desperately wanting to be a part of the "in" crowd must be part of the female makeup, he decided. He hadn't given two hoots for the popular clique. He'd formed his own crowd—the Blue Knights. None of them were class president or in the honor society, but for a bunch of kids who didn't have two red cents to rub together among the entire group, they'd garnered their share of respect.

Duke chuckled. Respect? Terror was closer to the truth. They looked tough and acted tougher. Worn Levi's, white T-shirts, and cheap blue vinyl jackets were their suits of armor, worn to protect them from the kids who could afford designer jeans with fancy labels and shirts with cute little polo players embroidered on the front. The Blue Knights had never done anything illegal, but their swagger as they stalked the school's corridors gave the impression they were only two steps from being the next Bonnie and Clyde of the Midwest.

None of his buddies were still around. Most of them had left Lumberton and never looked back, just as he had.

Once, he'd run into one of the Knights on a construction site. They'd shared a couple of beers and long, uncomfortable silences. Sure, they'd faithfully promised each other they'd get together and raise hell, but Duke hadn't seen the guy again. Neither of them wanted to renew an old acquaintance with their poverty-ridden background.

"There he is!"

Duke's head jerked up when he heard his sister's squeal of delight. He grinned, pushed away from the tree he'd been leaning against and waved. Bridget was the one person in the world he loved without reservation. He'd do anything for her, including eating a giant-sized serving of humble pie by returning to Lumberton.

"Hey, Duke, look at this," Bridget called. She handed her books to the girl next to her and Duke saw she was dressed in her cheerleader's uniform. She turned cartwheels, a back flip and landed in a full split inches from his feet.

"Not bad for a kid who crawled until she was four," he teased, pride ringing in his voice. He had picked up the tab for everything from the Reeboks on her feet to the perky silk scarf holding up her ponytail. It gave him great pleasure to give her things he'd never been able to afford.

Bridget took a playful swat at his leg as she bounced to her feet and hugged her brother. "Hey, guys," she called over her shoulder, "come on over and meet him. Doesn't he give new meaning to the word H-O-T!" She spelled this last word out, just as a cheerleader would at a game.

Slightly embarrassed by her enthusiasm, Duke dropped his arm over her shoulders and whispered, "Don't offer rides to the whole cheerleading team or you're gonna be late for work by the time we have a celebration dinner at McDonald's."

Her brown eyes widened in glee. "You got a job?"

Duke grinned and nodded.

"Where? Doing what?" she squealed, giving his neck another tight hug.

"You're choking the city's newest employee!" Duke said in a strangled voice filled with laughter.

"Mayor McMann hired you?" She grinned and winked. "I always said any woman mayor who rode a dirt bike to work didn't wear starched underwear."

Duke homed in on Jennifer's mode of transportation and ignored the underwear remark. It wouldn't be safe to let his mind dwell on whether her underclothes were starched. At the lake he'd wondered where she'd parked a car. He'd pegged her wrong. He'd thought she and her brother both drove matching Lincoln town cars.

While Bridget introduced her girlfriends, Collette and Lisa, Duke's mind remained on what a bundle of surprises Jennifer McMann had turned out to be. She certainly had a way of destroying his preconceived notions.

"...and he's gonna be living here until I graduate. Isn't that cool? I'd have him give you a ride on his Harley, but he's taking me out to celebrate!"

"What about Chad?" both girls chimed together.

"Chad who?" Bridget asked with an air of feigned disinterest.

"The boy you're trying to wangle an invitation to the prom from. That's Chad who!"

"Say-la-vee," Bridget replied. "That's French for 'frankly, my dear, I don't give a damn.'"

"Watch your mouth, kid," Duke warned.

"It's okay to quote literature." With a saucy flip of her hair and her hand tucked in the crook of her brother's arm, she sassed, "Even the mayor is reading *Gone with the Wind*."

"How do you know what she's reading?"

Bridget shrugged. "It fell out of her purse when she paid her check at the restaurant. She's always got a thick book in her purse."

Duke filed these tidbits of information about Jennifer along with the other things he'd learned as he waited patiently for his sister to exchange goodbyes with her friends. She eats at the Towne House Restaurant, where Bridget works, and she's an avid reader. Not earthshaking revelations, but for some unknown reason those tiny facts whetted his appetite to learn more about the mayor.

Bridget and Duke were munching on McDonald's French fries when he asked, "Does she date much?"

"Who? Lisa? She's a little young for you, don't you think?"

"Yeah, she's a babe in the woods, like you," he teased. "I was asking about Jennifer McMann."

Bridget squirted a packet of ketchup on the fries in the lid of her Big Mac. Through a fringe of inch-long lashes, she gave Duke a curious look. "You interested?"

"Maybe," he replied cagily. "We were classmates. I figured she'd have hooked up with Pete Howell, who was class president, or maybe Jack Hudson, the basketball star of our class. They were the kind of guys she dated.''

"Oh, yeah?'' She nibbled her fry. "Jack is married, living in Atlanta, teaching school, and Pete is an accountant in St. Louis. They're long gone.''

It didn't surprise Duke that his sister knew who, where and what about his classmates. Knowing your neighbor's business was better than getting free cable television.

"I don't think the mayor dates anybody from around here.'' She jabbed a potato into the thick, red sauce. "I don't know who she dated when she lived in Springfield before her dad got sick.''

Duke filed this new tidbit along with the others. "What was she doing in Springfield?''

"College, I guess. George graduated from Southwest M-O, didn't he?''

"M-O?''

"Missouri. You know, the abbreviation.''

Bridget's penchant for sprinkling spellings and poorly pronounced foreign words in her conversations often confused Duke, although he was getting used to it.

"Anyway, when her dad got sick, she moved back here. She inherited her parents' house over on Elm Street. Rumor is that before her dad died, he made her promise to run for mayor. She ran unopposed and stepped right into her father's shoes. Fin-ee.''

Bridget suddenly dropped the last bite of potato from her fingers, hastily wiping them on her paper napkin.

"Something wrong with the food?''

"No. Don't turn around and gawk, but that's Chad coming through the doors."

Purposely dropping his paper napkin on the floor, Duke reached to pick it up while checking out his sister's current heartthrob. Rust-colored hair, blue-eyed and freckle-faced, he looked and walked like the football quarterback that he was. Judging from the beeline he was making toward their table, Duke felt certain Chad wasn't in the throes of a Big Mac Attack.

Bridget groaned aloud and rolled her eyes.

Her reaction should have baffled Duke after the garbled telephone conversation she'd had with him last week. She'd sobbed her heart out to Duke on the telephone because Chad hadn't invited her to the prom. And if he did invite her, she was afraid it was only because of the rumors going around the locker room about a no-good Jones kid. And she couldn't go with him if he did really like her because she didn't have a long dress. And even if he did ask her and she did have a dress, she couldn't let him come out to the house. Jebediah was drinking heavier than usual; he'd embarrass her by screaming and yelling at Chad. Caught between having no prom date and what would happen if she did get a date, she'd been hysterical.

Like Duke, she'd suffered for being the Jones kid until the situation had become intolerable. This whole prom-date business was the final straw that broke the camel's back for her. She'd decided the only thing she could do was drop out of school and slink out of town in the dark of night. She'd called Duke to see if she could stay a few days with him.

Mixed-up, crazy kids, he'd thought. Both of us.

Their reasons were completely different, but Duke understood the need to run away. The compelling urge to flee combined with her emotional turmoil was a sure ticket to a dead-end road. He'd traveled that road. He wanted life to be easier for his sister.

He suggested she transfer her credits to the school district where he lived. She refused. Life would be just as bad with a new set of kids. She was going to drop out of school. Period. Only his promise to come home had forced her to unpack her bags. One way or another, he was determined to see her walk up the aisle and collect her diploma. Until then, he had to do everything within his power and influence to keep her in Lumberton.

"Can I have a word with you... alone?" Chad asked, his face stormy, shooting Duke killer looks.

"Chad, meet Duke."

Duke rose. Equal in height and build, Chad tried to assert his superiority as he shook Duke's hand. Familiar with this tactic, having used it, Duke grinned.

"Duke's my brother that lives in K.C., but he's come for a while."

Immediately, Chad's grip slackened. His ears turned bright pink; his freckles stood out as though they'd been dabbed on with a brown felt-tipped pen.

"Nice to meet you, uh, sir, uh, Mr. Jones."

"Everybody calls him Duke," Bridget chided, standing up beside Chad. "He isn't an O-L-D man."

"Yeah, well, I don't want to interrupt your supper, but I need to talk to your sister. It won't take long, I promise."

"Why don't I go get you a burger and fries? You can join us," Duke suggested, mentally counting the money in his billfold. If the kid had a hollow leg, he'd have to break another twenty. The benevolent big-brother role raised havoc with his streak of frugality.

"No, but thanks. I'm expected home for dinner."

Bridget led the way outside, with Chad on her heels and Duke cooling his heels.

He picked up a limp French fry soaked in ketchup, then dropped it. His anxiety on his sister's behalf was making his stomach turn flip-flops. The hamburger he'd eaten felt like a truckload of indigestible concrete.

True to his word, Chad escorted Bridget back to the table within minutes. From the look on their faces, whatever had happened pleased both of them immensely.

"See you Saturday, Bridget, after the baseball game."

She beamed Chad a sunshine smile. "Yeah, Chad. Saturday." Her smile faded the moment the doors swished behind him. "What am I gonna do?" she moaned. Tears shimmered in her eyes. She propped her head in her hands.

"About what?"

"My date! I'm gonna meet him at the game, but I can't let him take me home! You know what it's like at our house on Saturday night! Dad and his beer cronies will be playing poker!"

Cognizant of the abusive language those men could use and the level of intoxication by late Saturday night, Duke couldn't blame her for being ashamed. Duke had one advantage she didn't have: Jebediah hadn't spoken to him since he'd arrived. In fact, he'd made it crystal clear that his son wasn't particularly welcome.

"You could ask him to drop you off at my place," Duke offered. "Of course, you'll have to help me find a place first."

"An apartment? They don't exactly grow on trees around here." Her brow furrowed. "Wait a minute. I heard somebody mention that Mrs. Clarmont was thinking about taking in boarders. Golly, wouldn't that be great? Her husband left her that big Victorian house over on Elm Street."

His ears perked up when he heard the street name.

"Yeah!" she continued. "That's the ticket! Chad knows I live out in the boonies. I'll tell him I'm staying with you because it's so far home every night, what with cheerleading practice and work."

"Now wait a second...."

Bridget grabbed his hand. "You're the sweetest brother in the whole wide world! I love you to pieces."

Susceptible to his sister's loving praise, Duke merely grinned and nodded. Jebediah might protest against losing his housekeeper and cook, but what the hell. He'd have lost her for certain if she'd run off to join him in K.C.

"Can we go right now and see Mrs. Clarmont?" Not waiting for a reply, she dropped his hand and started raking the remains of his supper into the white paper bag. Her hands stopped when she glanced at her watch. "I can't go with you. I'll be late for work."

"I'll drop you off, then go see Mrs. Clarmont. Okay?"

"Better than okay. It's T-E-R-R-I-F-I-C!" she cheered.

* * *

Removing his silver-gray helmet, Duke let the motor idle while he glanced up and down the street. Appropriately, hundred-year-old elms lined it. The large, wooden frame houses had been built in the previous century, when materials and labor were cheap. To reproduce them for today's market would take tens of thousands of dollars, Duke figured. Even then, the old-world quality of the master carpenters it had taken to do the gingerbread work would be missing. A few of the yards needed tending, but overall, this was the nicest street in Lumberton.

He didn't belong here. That's why he hadn't turned off the engine. Bridget had really touched his soft spot to talk him into approaching his first-grade teacher for a place to live. Good Lord, Sophie Clarmont would take one look at him, remember who he was and why he left town and start hiding the family silver!

With one foot stationary, he wheeled his motorcycle around. He'd driven to the foot of the driveway when the sheriff's car pulled up and blocked his retreat.

Big Jim Elmo stepped from his car, his cigar clamped between his teeth, and shouted, "Hey, boy! What you doin' at the Clarmont house?"

The belligerent tone told Duke that the sheriff thought he was casing the house, preparing to burglarize it. His hostile insinuation rankled Duke's pride.

"I came to see Mrs. Clarmont."

"What for? You don't apply for welfare at her house!"

Duke's knuckles turned white from the grip he had on the handlebars. In a voice as deceptively calm as the eye of a hurricane, he quietly asked, "Are you placing me under arrest, sheriff?"

"Vagrancy is a misdemeanor. How much money have you got in your pockets?"

"I am not a vagrant."

"I reckon that takes some provin', huh?" One of Big Jim's hands settled on his holstered weapon. The red tip of his cigar flared; bluish-gray smoke streamed from his lips.

Duke remained astride his motorcycle, but he released the grips and folded his arms across his chest.

"I can cuff you and take you down to the police station, boy, or you can empty your pockets on the trunk of this here car."

Duke compressed his lips. He longed to tell Big Jim Elmo how he could buy and sell him with the money he'd saved and have plenty of change left over for a five-course meal. He'd be damned if he'd be humiliated by emptying his pockets.

"I've got a job."

"Oh, yeah? Who'd hire you?"

"Mayor McMann." A humorless grin twisted Duke's mouth as he heard the sheriff suck wind. "Why don't you radio over to city hall and check it out?"

"I reckon I'll just do that, boy."

One more smoke-crusted "boy" and Duke knew he'd be in danger of being fired before he started work. Jennifer wouldn't take kindly to his knocking the sheriff's teeth down his throat. He struggled to remain coolheaded as he listened to the radio conversation.

"Yeah, Bubba. This here's Sheriff Elmo. Call up to the mayor's office and see if she's done any hirin' lately. Jebediah Jones's kid says he's workin' for the city." He chuckled, then blew a smoke ring toward the windshield. "Yeah. I know it's a waste of time, but I gotta check out his story before I bring him in. Yeah. I'll wait."

Only a matter of seconds passed before Big Jim lurched against the steering wheel, coughed and wheezed. "Clementine said what! The mayor is where?" He paused. "Well, I'll be a ring-tailed polecat."

He'd been skunked all right, Duke mused, loving the sweet taste of passive revenge. Long after he'd shaken the dust of Lumberton off his shoes he'd still be grateful to Jennifer McMann for this one sweet moment.

Big Jim climbed from his car just as a vintage Buick pulled up behind the police car and honked.

"Miss Sophie, I'm glad you're here."

"You're blocking my driveway." Sophie stuck her arm through the window and waved at Duke. "Glad to see you, Duke. I hear you're going to be working for city hall!"

"Yes, ma'am." Grinning from ear to ear at her warm reception, Duke wheeled his Harley to the side to make room for her car. Purely for Big Jim's ears, he replied, "I start work tomorrow. Bridget said you're considering renting rooms. I'm looking for a place."

The cop car's engine revved; the tires squealed. Big Jim peeled away from the curb, lights flashing, siren squalling, heading toward the town square.

Duke swung off his motorcycle and opened the car door for Sophie. Worried that Big Jim would take his frustration out on Jennifer, he said, "The sheriff must have an emergency. Would you mind if I use your telephone?"

"To warn Jennifer?" Born and raised in Lumberton, Sophie knew exactly what had been taking place in her driveway: police harassment. "Why the surprised look, Duke? You must remember from being in my classroom that I have eyes in the back of my head and my ears to the ground." She grinned. "An awkward position for a woman my age."

"I'm afraid I've put Jennifer in a worse position."

"Come on in and call her."

Sophie spryly led the way into her house. Pointing to the phone she said, "The number is over the phone. While you're calling, I'll make certain the rooms upstairs are in order for you. Oh, yes, speak freely. I'm not on a party line."

"Thanks."

He dailed the number. The busy signal purred in his ear. His concern grew. How many others knew Jennifer had hired him and were hot under the collar? Until now, he hadn't considered what sort of problems hiring him had caused Jennifer. His concern had been to get a job. He redialed. Still busy. He clicked the receiver hook and placed his call again.

"Mayor's office, Clementine Gunther speaking."

"May I speak to Jen—Mayor McMann?"

"Who's calling?"

"Duke Jones."

"Oh!" Her voice changed from a bored tone to one of interest. "Duke! Her phone has been ringing off the hook since this morning. She's on the other line. Do you want to hold? Oh! Wait a second. Her light's gone out. I'll put you through."

Shifting from foot to foot, he made a snap decision: he'd offer to quit. His savings would shrink with no weekly income to balance out his expenditures, but he wouldn't let Jennifer take a bad rap for hiring him.

"Jennifer McMann speaking."

"Jenny? This is Duke." He paused. Diplomacy and tact were necessary. "I've reconsidered your offer to hire me for the vacancy in the maintenance department."

The immediate rush she'd felt when he'd spoken the nickname only her parents used and the quickening of her heartbeat at the sound of his voice lost impetus with his abrupt announcement. She'd been fending off frontal attacks; an attack from the rear guard was the last thing she expected.

"The paperwork is completed," she replied, her voice frosty. "You can't quit."

Duke raked his fingers through his hair. His voice dropped to a hushed level. "Jenny, you're taking criticism because of me. A job isn't worth it."

"It is if it's the only job in town...other than working for George."

"He refused to hire me. Why can't you do the same?"

"Because there's a principle involved here."

"What principle?"

"Fairness. It was the major thrust of my platform when I ran for office."

"Jenny, you ran unopposed!"

"And I was elected to run this town. Would it be fair to either of us if I listened to every busybody who calls me? Should I bow down to their whims? I know exactly what would happen. I wouldn't be able to do my job and you wouldn't have a job."

"Let's talk about fairness! Is it fair for them to crucify you? I'm the one they want to get rid of. Dammit, Jenny, I appreciate your being in my corner, but I can't let you take the heat for hiring me."

"You can't stop me. You can disappoint me, by not reporting to work first thing in the morning, but you can't stop me from expecting you to be there."

"Jenny, I promise, I'm not going to starve or be destitute without this job. I've got some money saved up. C'mon, lady, be reasonable. Just let it go."

"I am being reasonable and fair." She twisted the phone cord around her finger until she'd cut off the circulation above the second knuckle. She couldn't let him quit. For ten minutes she'd listened to the sheriff on one of his tirades. Duke would be fulfiling Big Jim's prophecy that he'd always been a shiftless, no-good bum and always would be one! "You do the same. I'm out on a limb. Don't saw it off behind me. Goodbye, Duke."

He glared at the receiver, then returned it to the hook.

Admiration for Jenny warred with annoyance that she had thwarted his act of unselfishness. She was a damned sight stronger and more obstinate than he had imagined. She couldn't possibly be the grown-up version of the quiet little teenager he remembered. Somewhere along the years she'd grown a steel backbone.

He questioned her fighting on his behalf as a battle of conflicting principles. Fairness versus unfairness? He shoved his balled fist into his pockets. She'd been raised in a silken cocoon, but any woman at her age had to know that life wasn't fair. Anyone naive enough to fight for justice would be waging a losing battle.

Furthermore, it was totally beyond his realm of comprehension to have such a staunch ally. She would have been smarter to go along with his adversaries.

Dammit! She should have let me quit!

"Frowns cause wrinkles, Duke," Sophie said, descending the steps. "I overheard the tail end of your conversation. Stop worrying about Jennifer. She's always been quiet and reserved, but that doesn't mean she's lacking spunk."

"I feel like I'm hiding behind her skirts. I'd rather be the town hellion than the town wimp!"

Sophie chuckled at the idea of this hunk of a man being considered a wimp by anyone. "You're confusing a job with gender. You're working for the mayor, not a woman. You wouldn't think twice about your manhood if her father had hired you."

"You're making me sound like a chauvinist."

"Are you?" Sophie peered at him through her bifocals as he shook his head. "No? Then why don't you let Jennifer do her job and you do yours? Now, let's get back to our business. Do you want to see the rooms or will you be leaving town?"

He'd be saving Jenny a lot of trouble if he left. But what about Bridget? An emotional eighteen-year-old would never understand why he'd reneged on his promise to stay in town until she graduated.

He had to stay, for his sister's sake.

"I'd like to see the rooms."

Chapter Five

I will not call the maintenance department and check up on him," Jennifer said, removing her fingers from the telephone.

In the past week she'd heard from half the town, but not a peep from Duke Jones. He could have at least sent a message via Clementine, she silently grumbled. Her secretary knew his whereabouts.

At the morning coffee klatch, Big Jim had detailed Duke's daily routine. Even Sophie relayed information about his comings and goings during the evening hours.

Everybody in town knows where he is and what he's doing but me. He could've called me.

Thoughts of Duke Jones hampered her concentration. At inopportune moments, like this morning during coffee klatch, she'd caught herself daydreaming. Sophie mentioned what a big breakfast eater he was; Big Jim said Duke and his sister had been seen suspiciously cruising around the deserted International Shoe factory on their way home from Bridget's part-time job. And all the while she'd been half-listening, she'd also been wondering if he'd been skinny-dipping at the lake since she'd last seen him.

Skinny-dipping!

The sight of his muscular shoulders and dark head slicing through the blue waters was a memory she should have delegated to the farthest back corners of her memory. Kodak film processors would have envied the clear mental picture she'd retained without the benefit of snapping a photograph.

My memory of that afternoon is like a videocassette player with an instant replay button, Jennifer silently groaned.

From the lake water coursing down his shoulders and chest to the drops clinging to those sinfully long eyelashes of his, from the aquamarine blue sky overhead to the spring green leaves on the trees, she'd replayed that picture in her mind dozens of times.

What bothered her most was how she'd realistically reconstructed his image while drastically changing her own behavior.

In her daydreams, her tongue-tied behavior radically changed. Her remarks to Duke were sophisticated and witty. Her feet weren't frozen to the rock where she'd stood. She'd waded into the water and dried his skin with her hands.

She could close her eyes and actually feel the lake water dripping from her fingertips; she could feel the heat emanating from his smooth supple skin. But that image wasn't what had her tossing and turning at night.

In the lonely confinement of her bedroom, her imagination ran wild. She'd dreamed of seeing his head slant over hers, his lips slowly draw closer and closer. She felt the warmth of his breath on her face, stirring a loose tendril of her hair. His dark eyes would glitter, then drift closed....

Damn! I'm doing it again! She pressed her hands against the side of her skull. Get out of my head. I don't want you there! I've too many things to accomplish—important things.

Determined to do something constructive, she slid a stack of unsigned letters in the center of the desk, picked up a pen and began signing them. She needed to direct the energy she wasted on her vivid imagination into finding a company willing to relocate to Lumberton.

"Clementine," she called, signing the last letter. "Bring me the tape for this morning's mail and run these over to the post office on your way to lunch, would you?"

Blowing her nails on one hand, Clementine held the tape between the thumb and forefinger of her other hand, being careful not to smear her newly polished nails. She dropped the tape and stared at the letters as though the paper would leap off Jennifer's desk and attack the fresh coat of nail polish.

"You didn't stuff the envelopes?"

"Appalling oversight on my part," Jennifer replied wryly. She swiftly folded, stuffed and sealed the letters. "Would you bring me a Quarter-Pounder?"

"I would, but I'm not going to McDonald's. I've been eating lunch at the Towne House."

"Didn't you tell me you hated their food?"

Clementine used the pads of her fingers to move the stack of envelopes until they were half on and half off the desk's edge. Carefully, very carefully, she clamped the stack between her palms. "I do hate it. Duke's sister works there."

"Not on the lunch shift," Jennifer blurted. "I mean..."

"I know what you mean. I don't get firsthand recounts of where he is and what he's doing, but the lunch waitress is a good friend of his sister. She told me that—"

"Never mind, Clementine." She might lack control over what took place during the morning coffee klatch, but she could control the flow of gossip in her own office! "Could you bring me a tuna fish salad sandwich?"

"He's one tough hombre to snag," Clementine commented, nodding her head. "I wish you'd have given him a job right here at city hall. I'm wearing my car out chasing him."

Jennifer smiled pleasantly. "There weren't any inside jobs available. Besides, you've wanted a new convertible. With all those miles you're putting on your Mustang, you'll have an excuse for your father to get you a new car."

"Jeez, you don't think I'd tell him where I've been going, do you?"

"Why wouldn't you?"

Clementine grimaced. "You'll know when you listen to the tape. I recorded his letter first and made a few suggestions on what you should tell him."

"He wants me to fire Duke, right?" Jennifer groaned, head in her hands.

"Dad has a friend who's a detective on the Kansas City police force. His friend is checking the files. Dad said in a couple of days he'll have the complete rundown on what kind of trouble Duke's been into recently. He doesn't recommend that you fire Duke, just have the sheriff watch him."

"Why?" Jennifer asked dryly. "Everybody in town is counting how many times he inhales per minute."

Giggling, Clementine moved the bundle of letters to her ample chest as they began to slip from between her palms. "You're the only woman in town who isn't interested in his whereabouts. Aren't you just a teensy bit curious?"

"I'm curious about whether I can get my tuna fish sandwich on rye or whole wheat bread."

She wouldn't deny or admit to being curious. Denying it would make her a liar; admitting it was out of the question.

"You'll be back by one o'clock, won't you?" Jennifer asked, glancing at her watch.

"I'll hurry."

Jennifer shook her head, following the east-west sway of Clementine's hips. How long did it take to eat lunch and get an earful of news? Surely an hour was sufficient.

She put the tape in the recorder, not bothering with the headphones since the office was empty.

"'Dear Mayor... It has been brought to my attention that a certain undesirable...'" came Clementine's bored voice.

Clementine inserted, "Who says he's undesirable, Dad? Everybody I talk to thinks Duke is *very* desirable!"

"'... element has recently entered the city limits of Lumberton. I have taken it upon myself to contact reliable friends in Kansas City...'"

"Cops," Clementine commented.

"'... to ensure the law-abiding...'"

"Stick-in-the-mud."

"'... citizens that we aren't harboring a dangerous felon. In my opinion, this person of questionable reputation could have been dissuaded from relocating if you had hired another qualified applicant. As a member of the city council, I felt it was my duty to inform you of my actions, which I took to counteract your questionable decision.'"

Jennifer pushed the eject button and inserted a fresh tape.

"Write a letter to Clementine's father. Standard heading, please. Dear Sir... According to the 'Policy and Procedural Manual for the City of Lumberton, Missouri,' it was my responsibility to interview and hire a qualified applicant for the city's maintenance department. In my judgment, Mr. Jones has adequate experience to warrant employing him. Should you have any specific complaints regarding his work, please direct them to me. Skip two spaces. Respectfully yours, four spaces, my name and office."

Jennifer swiveled around and propped her feet up on the windowsill. It was a good thing the tape was going to Clementine's typist friend, rather than directly back to Clementine. Otherwise, Jennifer would have had some choice comments to make about Clementine's dad that would have made his ears burn.

Clementine's father was a prime example of taking the boy out of the Ozarks but not taking the Ozarks out of the boy. He'd lived in Columbia, gone to college and to law school at Missouri University; he should have lost some of his hillbilly, down-home type of biases. When she was being fair she could excuse Big Jim for being narrow-minded because he'd never left the county. She couldn't excuse Clementine's father.

She'd had a bellyful of unsubstantiated accusations directed toward Duke. The townspeople had painted Duke as the devil reincarnated, just as they'd painted her as an angelic, naive nincompoop!

She was silently asking herself why they couldn't all just mind their own business when she heard a light rapping on her door. "Jenny, are you busy?"

The sound of Duke's whiskey-smooth voice jolted Jennifer from her seat. Caught off guard, she blurted, "Duke, come in. I was just thinking about you."

"Pleasant thoughts, I hope." He strolled into her office with one hand behind his back and nudged the door shut with his foot. "I heard Clementine mention to the waitress at the diner that she needed a tuna fish sandwich to go. I volunteered to deliver it."

She watched him place a napkin-covered paper plate in the middle of her desk. He was dressed in a khaki-colored work shirt and jeans, and she felt hard-pressed to think about anything as mundane as eating, not with him within touching distance.

"How nice of you," she said, remembering her manners. She gestured toward the oak chair in front of her desk. "Have a seat and tell me how the job is going."

"Well—" he folded at the waist and sat down "—I'm not here asking for a raise . . . yet."

Her heart thudded like a wild thing trapped in a cage as he shot her a devastating grin.

"Have you eaten?" She removed the paper napkin. "There's plenty here."

Duke swallowed, hard. Why did he feel as though there was something unbearably intimate in sharing a sandwich? It wasn't as though he would take a bite in the same place she'd just bitten. She'd take half; he'd take half. Nothing that should have made his mouth dry.

"No, but thanks. I've eaten."

The way he was hungrily eyeing her sandwich, Jennifer doubted it.

"You're sure you don't want half? There's plenty."

Why did her voice sound breathy, she wondered, as though she were Eve tempting Adam with a forbidden piece of fruit? It was just a tuna fish sandwich, and not a particularly appetite-inspiring sandwich at that. She picked the soggy slice of dill pickle off the bread; it left a damp, slightly green imprint.

"No. You go ahead. Sophie fixed me two sandwiches, potato chips and an apple for lunch. I'm afraid I'm going to get fat and lazy from pigging out on her lunches. I'm used to peanut butter and jelly on stale bread."

Automatically her eyes dropped to his trim waist. He followed the path of her eyes and sucked his stomach flat.

"We're neighbors, you know." Duke knew he was rattling on like a beat-up jalopy traveling over a washboard road. He could hear himself, but he couldn't stop. One moment of silence and he feared she'd politely excuse him from her presence.

"Elm Street," he said, his voice filled with awe. "Two Jones kids living on Elm Street. Pardon the bad grammar, but ain't America great!"

Jennifer opened her mouth to reply, but he continued his monologue. He's nervous! she realized suddenly. As nervous as a kid sent to the principal's office. Why, he's every bit as nervous as I am!

The only difference between their nervousness was that she'd learned to deal with her bouts of jangling nerves in elementary school. She remembered how her stomach had tied in knots as she listened to the other kids in the Roadrunners group stammer through an oral reading. Her serene composure had prevented anyone from ever suspecting that the finger she moved beneath the words was as incapable of comprehending the sounds as she was incapable of deciphering the words.

Then, like now, she sat and smiled and carefully listened as she watched the speaker's mouth move.

"I guess you know where Sophie lives. She's lived there forty years. Whew! Forty years in the same house." What was he doing talking about being in the same house for forty years as though he'd moved every six months? If he hadn't moved to Kansas City, he'd still be in the same tumbledown shack he was born in!

He kept on rattling faster and faster to cover up the flaw in his logic.

"Of course, you wouldn't consider that strange. You grew up in your house. I'll imagine you sleep in the..." his voice dwindled. He gulped. Good Lord, she ought to slap my face for admitting I thought about her in her bed. "Uh, work in the same room you used to do your homework in as a kid."

"Yes, I do."

He'd depleted his reservoir of small talk. Duke raked his hands through his hair. All week he'd mentally rehearsed telling her about small, funny incidents that had occurred on the job.

Why couldn't he remember them now?

He could barely think of anything other than how the sun rays coming through the window made a blond aura around her head that reminded him of a halo. Her blue eyes, intently watching him, drove lucid thoughts from his mind.

"Did I tell you how much Bridget loves living on Elm Street? She'd adopt Miz Sophie and live there permanently if she could."

"Sophie did mention how much she's enjoying having two young people at her house."

"Oh, yeah?" His face lit up, but he wondered if Jennifer was just saying that to be nice. "She likes Bridget turning up the stereo in the living room until the woofers vibrate the walls?"

"Woofers?" Jennifer grinned, and joked, "That sounds like two basset hounds howling from the insides of a record player."

Duke smiled. "The expensive stereo Sophie owns has woofers in its speakers. Better tone quality."

"Oh."

Duke rubbed the polished oak arms of his chair with his sweaty palms. What was he doing talking about Elm Street and Sophie's woofers? Jennifer took for granted the little homey pleasures that were new and exciting to him. He braced his arms and stood up.

The tiny bite of sandwich she'd taken expanded to the size of a live whale when she saw him preparing to leave. Her throat swallowed repeatedly to unblock the obstruction. She longed to ask him to stay but the words wouldn't form.

His hands smoothed the jeans on his upper thighs as he rolled to his feet. Casually ask her what she's doing this weekend? he mused. Casually? Ha! It's Friday. Too late to ask her out even if you could work up the guts.

"How's the job going?" Jennifer asked in a strangled voice.

"Good. Better than I expected."

"Meaning?"

"No one hassles me. That's good. They have a sit-back-and-wait-until-he-screws-up attitude. That's better than what I expected."

Jennifer put her own connotations on what he'd revealed. The men had ostracized him. They were treating him as though he were a time bomb ticking away, ready to explode. One minor mistake and they'd be able to point their self-righteous fingers at Duke and say, "We knew he'd make a mess out of everything—that's why we stayed away from him."

She hated stiff-necked hypocrisy. Those men could shrug off their mistakes, but woe be unto Duke if he so much as sneezed in the wrong direction.

"Everybody makes mistakes," she quipped.

"You don't." Duke saw the corners of her mouth tighten. Did she think she'd made a mistake when she'd hired him? Had he fouled up one of the piddly jobs he'd been assigned and not been told? "You haven't gotten a bad report on me, have you?"

"No."

Her shoulders sagged from the weight of his believing she was infallible. With time, he'd earn the respect of his fellow workers. The stigma of his past reputation would wane. Time wouldn't change her reputation as the fair-haired daughter of the town's oldest family who could do no wrong. It would continue to haunt her.

She wished she could tell him about the flaw she'd kept a dark secret. She couldn't. It would shatter the illusion he had of her. He'd think she was dumb. Nice but dumb. At all costs she didn't want Duke or anyone else to think of her as a dumb blonde.

The worried frown on his face made her push her own problem aside. She knew that the promise he'd made not to let her down had to be a burden on his peace of mind or he wouldn't have asked about a bad report.

"I made the right decision when I hired you, but that doesn't mean I don't make other mistakes. I do. I'm far from perfect, Duke."

In his eyes, she was a perfect lady. Sweet and pretty and smart, but most of all, she cared about people. She was the sort of woman he'd dreamed of, but he'd learned from a long line of disappointments to be a realist. Wanting to touch Jennifer was like crying for the moon—she was beyond his reach. She was too good for the likes of him.

With that thought in mind, Duke backed toward her office door. "I don't want to be late getting back to work. I'll see you."

"Yes." She added a few kilowatts to her wistful smile. "It's a small town. Our paths are bound to cross."

Unexpectedly, Duke stopped. He knew his place, but he'd always been a man who pushed boundaries. Three quick strides and he was opposite her with his palm extended upward. "Friends?"

She nodded, her heart aching for more than friendship. In slow motion, she lifted her hand and placed it in his. Their hands were as different as their backgrounds: his large, tough and calloused; hers smaller, soft and sensitive. His thumb wrapped around hers; her fingers curled around the base of his hand.

And as they touched, they both knew this was more than a handshake.

"Yes," she said softly. "Friends."

Duke turned her hand over and lifted her palm to his lips. Ever so lightly, he brushed a kiss on her heart line and then folded her fingers over it.

"Put it in your pocket and save it for when you're lonely."

A million dollars deposited in the city coffers wouldn't have given Jennifer the thrill of hearing what he'd said. Her eyes misted with happiness as she thought, tough exterior but he's sweet, sweet, sweet on the inside.

His lopsided smile and jaunty wave left her yearning for him to stay longer.

Jennifer stared at the empty doorway. A strange emptiness had settled in her stomach, pangs of hunger that wouldn't be appeased by eating the sandwich Duke had brought her.

He likes me, she mused, studying her closed hand.

Her heart warmed as she remembered the smile on his face when she'd agreed to be his friend. But somehow, she was unappeased by the lukewarm consolation of being liked or of being friends.

Jennifer shoved her chair until it wheeled to the window. From overhead, she watched Duke stride down the sidewalk.

His head dipped as he greeted Joe and Mabel Simpson, a retired farm couple. Distance made hearing what he'd said impossible, but she noticed whispers and over-the-shoulder glances being exchanged between Mabel and her husband.

Jennifer leaned forward, wanting to quiet their whispers by putting her hand over their mouths.

Her heart in her throat, she watched as he waved to someone inside her brother's grocery store. She blinked, unable to believe he'd waste his energy on waving at George. She wished she had X-ray vision and could see through the sunlight bouncing off the plate-glass window.

Kill 'Em With Kindness has got to be Duke's motto, she thought. How could anyone resist his winsome smile?

She admired his fortitude.

In his shoes, she'd have stuck her nose up in the air and pretended not to see the pointed fingers aimed at him or hear the hushed whispers.

He was trying so damned hard to make amends for the dirty trick of being born Jebediah Jones's son. She wished she could erase anyone's memory, removing the prejudiced blinders from their eyes so they could see him for the man he'd become.

Short of physically grabbing each and every one of them and shaking some sense into their heads, there wasn't anything she could do.

Jennifer sighed. She'd be his friend. Friendship was the only thing he'd wanted. Oh, yes, he'd kissed her hand to seal the bargain, but he hadn't asked her out. She sighed again, deeper and longer.

Friendship fell sadly short of her own desires.

Duke had indeed been waving at George, who stood at the checkout counter bagging groceries. Last week, he would have been more inclined to thumb his nose. But, feeling good about himself, he could afford to be nice to Jennifer's brother.

Whistling a happy tune from the old Broadway musical, he appeared as strong and mighty as the King of Siam. No one would suspect he cared two hoots for what people whispered behind his back. He'd grown up thinking half the town had laryngitis.

In all truthfulness, he didn't care anymore. He only cared what Jenny McMann thought of him.

She'd proven herself to be his staunch ally by taking the heat over hiring him. Now, she was his friend. He could make it through a gauntlet of verbal abuses as long as he clung to that thought.

Like everything else about her, Jenny had impeccable taste, he silently reasoned. If she liked him, he had to be worthy. Pure, undeniable logic, he thought, grinning inside and out.

He started jogging toward the back of the elementary school yard where the school's buses were parked. Because of his mechanical ability, he'd been "loaned" to the district's maintenance department to check the brakes on a couple of the buses.

By the ringing of the last bell, he promised himself he'd have those brakes fixed so they'd stop on a dime and give ten cents in change. They'd work perfectly.

Through hard, diligent work he'd get as close to perfect as a man could be. Then maybe, just maybe, he could impose on his new friend and ask her for a date.

Determined not to spend a beautiful Saturday afternoon with a dust mop in her hand, dressed in her grubbiest jeans and a Who T-shirt, Jennifer headed for the hills on her dirt bike. A few laps around the bike paths would clean the cobwebs from her brain.

More precisely, she hoped hot-lapping around the dangerous course and whizzing between the boulders and ruts would drive thoughts of yesterday's unsatisfying conversation with Duke from her mind.

She'd edited his one-sided monologue until she'd chucked it full of clever witticisms and bubbly laughter. The reality of her stilted replies had changed to sultry, irresistible come-ons. In her wildest fantasy, he'd said "lovers" instead of friends.

While she'd been mentally wrestling with changing their conversation, Clementine had returned to the office and told her she owed Duke for the tuna fish sandwich and chips. Clementine had fervently wished he'd paid for *her* lunch so she'd have a valid excuse to take him out for dinner.

Mercy, mercy, Jennifer thought, squeezing her gas throttle. She'd had to slap her hands to keep them from instantly picking up the phone, calling the maintenance department and leaving a message for Duke. My house. Eight o'clock. Bring your appetite and your jammies. Better yet, don't bring your jammies!

She chuckled at the reaction that message would have caused. Duke's supervisor would have had to be airlifted to Springfield for emergency medical treatment!

Although she'd enjoyed playing with the idea, she'd chickened out. Underneath her Midwestern, country girl wholesomeness was a Midwestern country girl who believed in love and commitment, not a sex-crazed, female vamp. It was okay to entertain wild flights of fantasy, but it wasn't okay to follow through on them.

She had placed a phone call, though—to the restaurant, to find out how much she owed Duke. Then she'd sent Clementine to the terrace level, with the money, to have Duke's boss put it with his paycheck.

Never let it be rumored that the mayor sexually harasses her employees!

Jennifer turned off the paved highway onto a dirt path too narrow to be called a road. This same path eventually led to the lake and her secluded cove, but she wouldn't be going there. At the fork in the path, she turned left instead of right.

Slowing her bike, she raised the smoke-colored glass on the front of her helmet. At the crest of a hill, she surveyed the ruts, curves and humps of the mile-long course. She knew them by heart. She'd spent many a Saturday afternoon here working out her mental frustrations, with only the Ozark Mountains to her left, the lake to the right and the difficult course dead ahead.

Adrenaline surged through her in anticipation of feeling her trail bike moving powerfully under her as she challenged the course. Admittedly, it was dangerous for a novice alone, but nothing made her feel more in control.

Here, the problems she faced were reduced to a simple equation: woman and machine against nature. Here, she had the solution to the problem—guts and fortitude.

Duke cocked his ear to the side when he heard the engine of a motorbike coming from over the hill. *Some kids must have discovered the racecourse I used to drive,* he mused, grinning.

None of his secret places were sacred. First, Jenny had discovered the best catfish hole in the county, and now, some kids were revving their engines, preparing to play Evel Knievel.

He didn't mind, but he was curious.

He checked the stringer line to make certain his morning catch of catfish were secured to the branch of the fallen tree submerged to the lake. His camping equipment, cooking utensils, bedroll and cane fishing pole were stashed in the trees lining the bank. Then he headed up the trail.

Winded from the climb and weaving through the trees at a rapid pace, he took a deep breath as he plunged through the brush near the track. What he saw froze the molecules of air in his chest.

The biker, crouched low over the handlebars, recklessly rounded the final curve, narrowly missing a tree, and goosed the gas throttle too much to avoid smashing into a ten-ton rock at the end of the course.

Arms raised, he bellowed, "Stop!"

Intent on beating her best time, Jennifer accelerated faster. She had three seconds before she'd have to brake or bail off her bike.

Three . . . two . . . ONE!

The bike's back wheel locked, skidding sideways; her rubber-soles shoes dug into the loose soil. In a cloud of dust, she stopped with one foot braced against the base of the boulder. Her bike leaned precariously in the opposite direction while Jennifer glanced at her stopwatch.

She'd shaved a few tenths of a second off her past record. Delighted, she yanked off her helmet, tossed it high in the air and crowed, "All right, Jennifer McMann, you beat your record!"

"You almost broke your fool neck!"

Startled by Duke's voice, she lost her balance. The weight of her dirt bike pushed against her right thigh and pulled her foot off the rock. The next thing she knew, she'd been yanked off the seat and jerked against a massive chest, solid as the rock where her foot had rested.

Duke tightly cradled her face against his chest; his arm looped around her waist. Blood pounded in his ears from the fright she'd given him.

She could've been badly hurt, was his only lucid thought in a jumble of expletives.

"Did you see me?" Jennifer asked, her face flushed, her blue eyes gleaming with victory. Content to be in his arms, it didn't cross her mind to let him know she'd recovered her balance. "I beat my record."

"You also scared a year's growth out of me."

Their waists, hipbones and thighs were touching. His scowl changed into a wide smile as she looped her arms around his neck and hugged him. She felt good in his arms, not too tall and not too short, slender but not too thin. She was all woman—one helluva woman!

Chapter Six

A man can't have any privacy in Lumberton, can he?" Duke teased, lightly feathering a wisp of hair behind her ear.

Suddeny aware of how she'd draped herself around Duke, Jennifer wiggled from his arms. "Are you referring to my racetrack?" she countered.

"Your racetrack?" His dark brows winged upward. "You were shaking pom-poms in the high-school gymnasium when I earned the money for a secondhand motorcycle." Pom-poms weren't the only thing she was shaking, he mused as she bent over to right her bike. To avoid tormenting himself by staring at her, he moved to her side. "Here, let me help."

"I always thought it was a shame you weren't in the sports program." She stepped aside and watched the play of muscles beneath his shirt as he lifted her bike off the ground and propped it against the boulder. Her tongue curled in her mouth, threatening to tie into a knot and leave her speechless. Determined not to be a tongue-tied dolt, she lifted her face toward the cloudless sky.

Duke shrugged. Sports cost money. Their small high school lacked the funds to buy all the equipment needed. The parents made up the difference. The Joneses didn't have that kind of money.

"Sports are a good means of venting frustrations."

"Is that what you were doing when you put blisters on my obstacle course?"

"Yeah." She grinned, giving him a sidelong glance, then widening her eyes and batting her eyelashes. "You'd have made a great jock."

"Madam Mayor, you're flirting with danger... again."

She swung her arms open wide and twirled around on one foot. "I'm not afraid of anything out here. This is my little corner of the world."

Duke watched her impromptu dance, fascinated by her lack of inhibitions. He felt in touch with her spontaneity. There had been countless times he'd jumped for joy and clicked his heels in the very place where she stood.

Freedom.

No one owned the great out-of-doors. Away from prying eyes and wagging tongues, he knew no fear. He felt free to be the real Duke Jones.

He pondered the idea that this adorable, vibrant imp twirling in front of his eyes was the *real* Jennifer McMann.

Pleased by the effect the natural setting had on her, he thought, this is my place—her place—our place. Out here, they weren't restricted by the past . . . or the future. Here, they weren't restrained by what people saw them as being. They were simply a man and woman sharing the unspoiled beauty of a spring day in the Ozark Mountains.

Jennifer grabbed his hand and tugged him along with her. "I'll bet you've been skinny-dipping, haven't you?"

"Nope."

"Lordy, I'm hot and dusty!"

Duke balked. As he was the stronger of the two, Jennifer had to slow her steps to match his. "I've got some iced tea. That'll quench your thirst."

"My thirst, yes, but it won't get the grime off me." A mischievous grin curved her mouth. Before she'd left the house, she'd prepared to take a swim by wearing a two-piece bathing suit under her shirt and jeans. "I can hardly wait to cannonball off the rocks into that deep pool under the cliffs."

She dropped his hand and dashed toward the lake.

"You'll ruin my fishing," he muttered, dragging his heels.

Concern for their friendship worried him far more than catching catfish. The chances of their having a friendly romp in the water were slim. He considered his strong will as being akin to tempered steel, but even steel would snap if too much pressure was put to bear on it.

"C'mon, slowpoke," Jennifer called over her shoulder. Her fingers busily yanked at the hem of her T-shirt. "Last one in is a scaredy-cat!"

Duke shut his eyes—the gentlemanly thing to do. They popped open of their own accord, just in time to see Jenny dart through the trees, waving her shirt over her head like a flag of surrender.

"Better a scaredy-cat than a cooked goose," he mumbled aloud.

There was no way in hell he could go skinny-dipping with her. His physical response to seeing her naked would be far stronger than his willpower. The water was cold but not *that* cold!

"You go ahead," he called. "I'll gather some firewood."

"Party pooper!"

Her good-natured taunt echoed through the trees. He could feel the sweat rolling down the side of his face. Duke seldom turned down a dare. His fingers fiddled with the buttons on his shirt.

If the shock of diving into the pool of ice water didn't kill her, seeing him buck naked would!

His fingers trembled, stopped moving, then flicked the button loose. He'd change into the cutoff jeans he'd brought along to wear back into town tomorrow. They weren't the sort of snazzy swimwear he wore to the apartment-complex pool back in Kansas City, but they'd do for a swim in the lake.

Relieved to have found a solution to his problem, he picked up the pace of his steps until he was running after her. He heard a splash as he began to scramble down the deep embankment at the lake's edge. By the time he collected his cutoffs from his backpack, her head bobbed to the surface of the water.

"Beatcha!" she chortled with glee. "You have to let me dunk you as a forfeit." She stood up and he saw she was wearing a red bikini. It was skimpy, but she certainly wasn't nude.

"Uh-uh, lady. I didn't agree to letting you drown me!" He shook his shorts in her direction. "Anyway, you cheated. You must have had a suit on already. I'll be back in a minute."

"You'd better hurry. This water has icicles in it!"

Duke bit his tongue to keep from suggesting that she bake her bones in the sunshine to get warm. The thought of returning to find her lazing on the flat rock near the lake's edge had the sweat pouring down his chest.

You won't touch her, he silently coached himself while hurriedly shucking his clothes. A little splish-splash, a quick dunk and a mad dash out of water— that's it! Anything more, and you'll be like a kid playing with matches. Poof! Up in smoke! End of friendship! Kaput!

He tugged his shorts up his legs, hiking them up until the snap was an inch beneath his navel.

"C'mon! My teeth are starting to chatter!" he heard as he gave a final pep talk to himself. "Here I come! Ready or not!"

He charged from under the cottonwood tree bellowing a mighty Tarzan yell. Wishing he had a vine to swoop down to the water on, he settled for using the flat rock as a platform. His hands arched in front of him; he dove in headfirst, barely missing Jennifer.

Laughing at his antics, Jennifer swiped water from her face and waited for his head to emerge. She'd given him time to catch his breath, then she'd collect the forfeit he owed her. Her eyes skimmed the water's surface.

Where was he?

The question had barely popped into her head when she felt his hands on her ankles, her feet being pulled from under her. Too late to prevent his playful attack, she flailed her arms, shrieked, "Unfair!" and catapulted backward.

Duke swam to waist-deep water. Quicker than a master carpenter driving a penny nail, he emerged from the lake. Proud of himself for adhering to his restrictive hands-off policy, he stretched out on the flat rock and assumed a pose of complete innocence.

"That was an ornery trick, Duke Jones." Only the laughter in her eyes betrayed her pretense of being indignant. Her palm rippled across the water, splashing him. "You get back in here!"

He lay perfectly still as though sound asleep. His lips barely moved as he whispered, "I'd say we're even. It was ornery of you to make me think you were going skinny-dipping, wasn't it?"

It was. She couldn't deny it.

"Wanna race?"

"Nope."

"Wanna see who can hold their breath the longest under water?"

"Nope."

"Wanna swim between my legs?"

Duke groaned; Jennifer blushed.

"No!"

"Well, what are you going to do? Just lie there and get sunburned?"

He opened his eyes and cast her a naughty wink. "I'm contemplating frying the catfish you're about to squash with your feet."

Her eyes dropped to the near-transparent water. Sure enough, there were four dark shadows lazily fanning their pectoral fins within inches of her toes. "Where'd you catch them?"

"That's a deep, dark secret."

"Your secret would be safe with me," she bargained. "I'm the world's worst fisherman."

"Jenny, I'd rather tell you my savings account number than divulge the location of my honey hole."

He rolled to his side and held out his hand for her to lever herself up beside him.

Jennifer grinned. This was her big chance to collect his forfeiture. She braced her foot at the base of the slippery rock and linked her hand around his wrist. One mighty tug later, she giggled with delight as he rolled into the water.

"You stinker! Innocent blue eyes and a fiendish heart!"

He lunged at her; she dodged sideways. Water surged between them, lapping over her shoulders. While he struggled to restore his balance, she puffed her cheeks with air and dived under water. Eyes open, she grabbed him around the knees; her shoulder pushed against his thighs. She had expected him to collapse backward as she had, so she felt like a ninety-pound weakling when he didn't bulge.

She gulped her reservoir of air and pushed harder, to no avail. His tactic didn't work for her. She'd have to improvise. With her air supply rapidly depleting, she had to think of something fast.

Light-headed from being near oxygen starvation, she thought, I could yank the fringed hem of his cutoffs. That would buckle those knees of his. And yours, too, she tacked on as an afterthought.

Duke curtailed her vengeful thoughts by yanking her upright against him. Her arms were around his neck; his were around her slender waist. Before either of them realized they were intimately embracing, they were laughing, gasping for air.

"Give up?" Duke chuckled.

"Never. Not until you tell me where you caught those fish! I won't dunk you if you tell where you caught them."

Her barely clad breasts bobbed against his bare chest. A shiver of response made Duke clamp his hands on her waist to pry her loose. He broke the grip her arms had on his shoulders; they straightened, but her fingers clung to his neck. Her legs automatically circled his waist to get into position to dunk him.

Her skin, smooth as silk, defied his resolution not to touch her. He couldn't help but notice that his hands almost completely circled her waist or that the soft swell of her breasts were mere inches from the tips of his thumbs. It wasn't frolicking in the water or physical exertion that shortened his breath or sent a shaft of heat coursing through his veins; it was the sweet enticement of the calves of her legs holding them together.

He valiantly tried to stop his natural reaction by gritting his teeth and looking upward into the sun. One by one he mentally willed his fingers to slacken their hold. He valued her friendship. Gut level, he knew his overwhelming response to her would demolish their friendship to smithereens. Once destroyed, he'd never be able to put it back together again.

Without looking at her, Duke felt the moment Jenny became aware of his concentrated effort to separate them without offending her. His chin dropped until their eyes met. Her eyes widened. She blinked. The dark centers of her eyes flared wide. She kicked her legs and dropped her hands. In two seconds flat, she'd broken his light hold on her waist by kicking her legs and dropping her hands.

Jennifer shivered. The skin on the palms of her hands and inner thighs tingled from his body heat. If the laws of physics were accurate, a cloud of steam should have arisen. She edged backward until she felt her backside touch stone. She'd literally caught herself between a rock and a hard place.

"Sorry," she mumbled, briskly rubbing the goose bumps peppering her upper arms.

Rightly accused of teasing him about going skinny-dipping, she felt guilty as sin for pulling him into the water. Did he think she'd attempted to dunk him to physically tease him? She hadn't reached the ripe age of twenty-six without knowing what a man thought of a female tease.

He misread the anxious look in her eyes as fear. "Jenny, don't be afraid of me. Don't apologize, either. I'm the one who's habitually in the wrong." He ran his fingers through his wet hair as he searched for words to close the widening breach in their friendship. He couldn't bear the thought of her walking away from him, rejecting his friendship. His hand whipped against the lake's surface. "Why do I keep messing up the few good things that come along in my life?"

"What happened wasn't your fault," she refuted, unable to let him take the blame for the sexual tension that had strung tightly between them. Thoroughly disgusted with herself, she moved toward the shoreline, muttering, "I'm the one who can't be content with just friendship."

"What'd you say?" He couldn't believe his ears. Using his hands to help propel him forward, he closed the space between them.

Jennifer stepped from the water and grabbed her shirt from the ground. She hastily dried her arms and face. "You heard me."

"Yeah, but I'm having trouble believing it." He caught her shirt in his hand and yanked downward until he could look into her troubled eyes. "I'm not good enough to be your friend, much less anything else."

"Don't talk to me about who's good and who's bad!"

Tears welled in her eyes. Everyone in town, except for Sophie, Clementine and his sister, maligned him. And those very same people who were so quick to render judgment against Duke Jones thought sweet Jennifer McMann was virtue personified. She felt an overwhelming need to correct that misconception. Her lips worked soundlessly as she tried to reveal the secret she'd kept hidden for years.

"Don't cry, Jenny." When Bridget cried, he'd fold her into his arms to absorb his sister's pain. Jennifer wasn't his sister. He couldn't trust himself to hold her in a brotherly fashion. Uncertain of how to comfort her without touching her, his arms stretched out toward Jennifer as he stepped backward. "I'm not worth the salt of your tears."

"Stop it, Duke." Her knuckles swiped beneath her bright eyes. "Stop telling me how unworthy you are. So you made mistakes as a kid. Big deal! Is your past reputation contagious? If I touch you, is it going to rub off on me? Make big black marks on my soul? Tarnish my halo?"

A mockingbird trilled from a branch of the cottonwood tree nearby. Somewhere in the far distance, its mate called a mournful reply.

As naturally as the birds responding to one another's spring mating calls, Duke took a giant step forward and wrapped his arms around her shoulders, drawing her against his chest.

"Shut up, Jenny."

"I won't shut up. It infuriates me to hear you put yourself down."

"Then I'll shut up. Okay?"

She shook her head. "No. Just tell me why you think you're going to mess up with me...without trampling on your self-esteem."

"Ah, Jenny, Jenny, Jenny," he crooned softly next to her ear. "You've known about me almost all of my life. What can I tell you that you don't know?"

Her cheek flattened against the thick mat of dark hair on his chest. She raised her hand and placed it over his heart. "What's happening in here? Open up. Let me inside."

He felt as though his heart swelled beneath her hand. No one had ever cared enough to probe beneath the layers of thick skin he'd grown to shield his vulnerable heart. He honestly didn't know where to begin peeling off the layers of hurt.

"You'd better sit down," he suggested, holding her hand and crossing to the flat rock at the water's edge. He squatted down Indian style and watched as Jennifer gracefully dropped down beside him. All the while, he dug deep into his memories to find the root of his troubles.

When did they begin? He could scarcely remember a time when he wasn't in one kind of trouble or another.

"I must have been four, maybe five years old, the first time I realized the Jones family wasn't like other families. I guess living so far from town and not being around other children and their parents, I must have thought everyone's dad lay around the house all day drinking whiskey, watching ball games on television, passing out on the sofa before sunset. And every mother cooked and cleaned and hid their kids behind their skirts to protect them."

Jennifer stiffened, as though physically struck by one of his father's physical blows.

"Believe it or not, that wasn't as bad as it sounds. To me, dodging his clumsy swipes was like you playing peekaboo with your father. It's a game, a way of getting your father's attention. It didn't hurt."

She kept her mouth shut so as not to interrupt the flow of thoughts, but she inwardly shuddered over his father's neglect.

"What hurt was realizing everyone didn't live like the Joneses. Other fathers had jobs. They earned money to buy nice things for their families—just like the fathers on television. I remember asking my mother why my dad didn't work. She made excuses for him. When I asked him, he came unglued. I spent that night in the woods, curled into a ball, wondering why we were different than other folks.''

He took a sidelong glance at Jennifer. She'd wrapped her arms around her legs and was staring across the water, but he knew she'd heard him. He knew from the grim expression on her face that he should stop. Maybe make a joke. But now that he'd started, he wanted her to understand where he'd come from, why he viewed the world through jaundiced eyes and how he'd acquired the strength to stand alone.

''My mother dropped out of school in sixth grade, but she was a great believer in education. At six, when I entered Miss Sophie's first-grade class, I wanted to be the smartest kid in the class.''

''You were a Cardinal,'' Jennifer said softly. ''The top reading group.''

''Uh-huh. That lasted as long as it took my mother to pack a grocery sack full of clothes and leave. By third grade I'd learned hawks fly faster than doves. Troublemakers get more attention than good kids. By junior high, my motto was Tough Kids Don't Bleed, at least nobody dares to cross them to find out if they bleed. I wasn't just the Jones kid, I was *the* Jones kid.''

He gave a dry laugh that lacked humor. ''And all the while I was swaggering down Main Street, I was scared. Scared I was going to be just like my father. Scared to set my sights on amounting to something and fall short. I'd have nightmares where I'd see people shaking their heads and saying, 'He's Jebediah Jones's kid. A chip off the old block.' Isn't that ironic?

I strutted down Easy Street and set myself up for failure with each step I took. What's even more ironic is that I didn't realize I was carrying a 'chip off the old block' on my shoulder like a badge of courage!''

Jennifer looked at the hard, uncompromising line of his jaw and was grateful he continued to stare blindly across the lake. From the acid bitterness in his voice, she knew that what he'd bottled up had been eating at him for years.

It was just as well that he didn't look at her. One of his glances would reduce her to tears. To help him, she had to be strong.

"By the time I was sixteen, I must have unconsciously decided that I had to make my mark somehow." His lashes lowered as he thought, this will make her understand why we can only be friends. Unmercifully, he said, "I went to your father's store and stole something I didn't *need* for survival—peppermint candy canes. He caught me red-handed and had me arrested, to teach me a lesson." Again he gave a dry laugh. "The juvenile authorities put me in my father's protective custody."

Aghast to learn it had been her father who'd played an important role in Duke's troubles and that they'd placed Duke under his own father's care, Jennifer placed her hand on his arm. His biceps flexed involuntarily as though to shake off her sympathetic touch. "My father and the juvenile court system made a grave mistake," she said softly. "You should have been getting protection from your father!"

"In all fairness, your father did point out the error in judgment the judge had made, but the juvenile judge, who'd just been elected, covered the whole county and didn't know about Jebediah Jones. The judge probably thought he was being charitable to a first-time offender. I didn't want his charity any more than I wanted the welfare checks that supported my old man's alcoholism. So...I hightailed it out of town and went to Kansas City.''

"Where you made something of yourself," Jennifer concluded, desperately wanting Duke's story to have a happy ending.

"Where I nearly starved to death," he replied drolly. "I hung around an apartment-complex construction site and made enough money to buy food. At night, I'd sneak past the guard and sleep in one of the finished apartments. The rest you know. It was on my application form."

Jennifer worried her lower lip with her front teeth. Should she tell him that she didn't know anything other than what he'd told her during his interview? He'd shared confidences with her. He'd trusted her by telling her the worst there was to know about him.

She should have felt at ease telling him her awful secret. There was one main difference that kept her lips tightly sealed. He'd left town and made something of himself; she'd stayed in town and lived a lie.

Much as she wanted to unburden her guilt, she kept her mouth shut.

He'd waited for a response from Jennifer. When none was forthcoming, a shaft of disappointment cut him to the quick. He picked up a stone and flung it into the water, feeling like a kid who'd reached for the candy canes and had his hand slapped.

He'd asked too much of her. Dammit, he should have known better than to spill his guts. She probably thought less of him now than when he'd bullied his way into her office and demanded to be hired. At least back in her office he'd kept his pride intact. He hadn't begged for compassion or hung his dirty laundry out for her inspection.

"I can't change who I was, but I have changed who I am," he said with a determined ring in his voice. He rose to his feet and hooked his thumbs in the belt loops of his cutoff jeans. "I'm my own man. I don't ask for anything I haven't earned and I don't want for things I don't need for survival."

His uncompromising stance told Jennifer that she'd unintentionally offended him. She scrambled up, wretched at the thought of being insensitive, wanting to make amends for her shortcomings.

"I'm proud of the man you've become."

His head snapped around. "You are?"

"That's why I wanted to hear everything from your viewpoint. Your reputation didn't match up with the kind of man I admire. But *you* do. Your past is behind you. I'm expecting great things of you in the future."

Jolted, Duke stared at her. She admired him? She didn't think less of him or hate him? He studied her eyes to make certain she wasn't just saying that to be nice. He could spot a lie. A liar's eyes would shift to the side; her eyes steadily met his. They were as clear of untruths as the blue heavens above them.

Happiness such as he'd never known rushed through him. He must have changed if Jenny McMann admired him. He wanted to hug her, swing her around and around, laughing with joy.

Jennifer grinned as she watched his mouth lift in a crooked smile. "I don't suppose I could talk you into sharing your catfish dinner with me, could I? We could take your catch to my house and fix them."

Laughing aloud, Duke was pleased by her invitation, but he wasn't foolish. She might have forgiven him for his past; the others in town distinctly remembered it.

"Why don't we fix them here?" He pointed to the knapsack containing the camping equipment he'd brought to the lake. "There's nothing better than fresh fish fried over an open fire."

Entranced by the sun rays dancing in his dark hair and the infectious grin molding his lips into a warm smile, Jennifer could think of a hundred things better than fried fish, but she was content just being with him.

"I'd love it."

A thought she should have squelched barged into her mind as she watched Duke hustling toward his backpack. I could fall in love with him. Sound reason prevailed. She could fall for him, but she wouldn't.

Duke Jones had earned his freedom; she was still shackled by the chains of illiteracy.

She couldn't leave Lumberton and succeed, as he had. She'd tried . . . and failed.

During the few months she'd been in Springfield, she'd learned that lesson. Street signs, maps, directions, little things Duke would take for granted, were beyond her comprehension. She had been totally lost.

He had no idea how she'd admired him for being able to do the simple task of filling out an application form. She'd had to ask a stranger for help. The woman had looked at her as though she were mentally deficient. She hadn't had the nerve to say, "Hey, I'm not dumb. I just can't read." The lady would never have believed her—everybody with a nickle's worth of sense could read.

Humiliated, she'd taken a menial job that didn't require being able to complete an application form. A menial job for menial pay, she thought, remembering how her father had supplemented her meager income. And all the while, everyone in town believed she'd enrolled at the state college or was attending the business school in Springfield.

It was almost a blessing in disguise when her father had become ill and needed her at home. No one asked any questions because everyone assumed that good, sweet Jennifer McMann had returned home to be at her father's side during his illness. Only the small blessing had become a disaster when her father told her he was dying. He'd insisted that she run for his office as mayor. Unable to refuse him anything, she'd confessed her secret and let him fill out the necessary forms.

Her thoughts deep inside her past, she watched Duke lug his cooking utensils back to the shoreline.

Duke Jones could cast aside his past reputation and thrive in the outside world. Without her reputation to protect her, Jennifer McMann would be a failure.

Yes, she could fall in love with him, but he wouldn't return her love if he knew the truth about her.

Chapter Seven

Why'd you come back?" Jennifer asked as she licked the tartar sauce off her index finger.

As he'd promised, the fried fish were the best she'd ever eaten. She greedily eyed the sizzling fillet he'd speared from the iron skillet and placed on the plate they shared.

"Go ahead, Jenny. There's plenty."

He rolled another fillet in the cornmeal, flour and pancake mix combination and dropped it into the hot oil. He frowned, thoughtfully considering giving her a flip answer. Jenny was a good listener; she made him want to share his problems. That might be a bad habit to get into, he mused, knowing how much lonelier he'd be when he went back to his solitary life in Kansas City. What the hell, he decided, completely lowering his guard.

"Bridget was considering dropping out of school before graduation."

From what Jennifer had heard from Clementine, Bridget was a cheerleader, a good student, popular with the other kids. Her appetite waned at the thought of one more of Lumberton's finest anxious to start her life away from her hometown.

"There's not much future for her here," Jenny admitted reluctantly. "Between the shoe factory and the marble quarry shutting down, the governor should have declared Lumberton an economic disaster area."

Duke nodded his agreement. "True, but that isn't her main concern. Who will ask her to the prom is at the top of her priority list. She thinks she's madly in love with Chad Felton."

"He's a good kid, too. Is he interested in her?"

"Oh, yeah, but Bridget knows the Feltons disapprove of their darling son getting entangled with her."

Jennifer knew the Feltons well. They were down-to-earth farmers, making a living tilling marginal soil. They weren't rich by any stretch of the imagination.

"Maybe she's being oversensitive."

His dark eyebrow rose with skepticism.

"Chad earned a scholarship to the Rolla School of Mines," Jennifer pointed out. "I can understand why his parents wouldn't want him to get emotionally involved with any girl."

"'Emotionally involved' being a nice way of saying getting a girl knocked up and trapping a boy into a shotgun wedding?"

She dropped the fillet on the plate. "No."

Ashamed of himself for bluntly saying what others around town politely whispered in hushed voices, he muttered an apology.

"Stop acting as though I have virginal ears, would you? I'm not a throwback to the eighteenth century."

"You're a liberated woman, right?"

"Right. No bustle. No high-button shoes. No hoopskirts."

"Great." He rocked back on his haunches and looked her straight in the eye. "Then take a walk in my sister's Reeboks. What would have happened if I'd asked you to our prom? Wouldn't your father have put up a stink that could've been smelled in St. Louis?"

"That's different," she automatically protested, feeling her toes curl at the thought.

She'd gone to the senior prom alone. Not exactly alone, she silently amended. Her father had been her escort. The mayor always attended the prom, so it had been natural for her father to be her escort. Or at least that's how her father had rationalized it when he'd found her cloistered in her bedroom, sobbing her heart out because no one had asked her to the prom.

"The Jones kid and the mayor's daughter," Duke said, sarcasm dripping more heavily from his words than the tartar sauce that made white blobs on the plastic plate. "You're right. That would be different."

"Dammit, Duke. You never took a second look at me."

"Wrong. I looked. I knew better than to touch. You were one heck of a lot more valuable to your father than a stringer of candy canes."

"What a backhanded compliment!" Her face tingled as though it had been slapped. "You didn't have the gumption to ask me for a date. You don't know for certain how I'd have responded, do you?"

Back then, Duke had never been able to resist a dare; now, he was hard-pressed to ignore her challenge. "How about dinner next Saturday night?"

"I accept."

The heat caused by flared tempers instantly cooled.

"You do?" Duke asked, genuinely amazed, both by his audacity and her acceptance.

Jennifer grinned at his look of astonishment. Accepting a date with Duke would complicate her life, but she'd sort through those complications later.

"Why are you surprised?" She pointed to the plate she'd scraped clean. "I've been an absolute glutton eating your fish."

"But, Jenny, being seen together in public with me is different than sharing a meal over a camp fire."

"So? What are you doing? Asking me out in one breath and canceling our date in the next breath?" Speaking of breathing, she realized hers had become decidedly irregular. Injecting a light note, she added, "I promise not to seduce you and demand a formal wedding—white shotgun and all the trimmings."

Her questions and promises were like tiny arrows shot from Cupid's bow aimed at his heart. She had absolutely no idea how her smile affected him. He felt as though he'd swallowed the sun and was glowing all the way through. He knew if he tried to tell her how she made him feel he'd sound sappy.

"Six o'clock?"

"You've got a date."

The following Friday evening, Duke sat in a booth at the Towne House Restaurant watching the evening dinner rush. Only in Lumberton could two families eating chicken-fried steak qualify as a rush.

He leaned forward to glance down the sidewalk toward city hall. Silently he cursed the urge to get a glimpse of Jenny. The entire week he'd practically skulked around town to avoid meeting her face-to-face. Each time the phone rang at Miss Sophie's, he'd known with fatalistic certainty that it was Jenny calling to make an excuse for breaking their date.

His hand went to the sealed envelope in his front shirt pocket. Positive it was merely a matter of time until Jenny came to her senses and canceled their date, he'd been afraid to open his paycheck envelope. She'd paid him back for her tuna fish sandwich via his paycheck envelope, hadn't she?

He pulled the envelope from his pocket and held it up to the light streaming through the plate-glass window. There was definitely a note in there, and the writing looked feminine—rounded with curlicues.

"Payday?" Bridget swiped the watery imprint of his iced tea glass off the Formica tabletop. She snatched the white envelope from between his fingers. "Can I borrow five dollars until tomorrow, when I get paid?"

Duke visibly paled. Whatever flimsy excuse Jennifer had written, he didn't want his sister to read it.

"Hey, I was only kidding." She dropped the envelope next to his plate. "I know you have to pay the weekly rent. If you're running short you can have my paycheck. I don't need a silly old lipstick."

With the envelope safely back in his pocket, Duke said, "I told you not to worry about money." Conscious of the preparations she'd been making for her big date with Chad, Duke teased, "You've found a tube of lipstick that perfectly matches the crimson red lettering on your cheerleading uniform?"

"How'd you know?"

"I'm not deaf. I heard you and Miss Sophie giggling as you plotted your strategy at the breakfast table. Do you realize you two have more lipstick stripes on the backs of your hands than a tribe of Ozark Indians on the warpath? Let me give you a tip...."

"It's about time you tipped me." She held out her hand and gave him a cheeky grin. "I've been waiting on you every night and I haven't seen so much as one thin dime."

He reached for his wallet with one hand and for the paper sack beside him in the booth with the other. "I meant tip as in brotherly advice."

"That's not a tip—that's a lecture."

"Since when have I started lecturing you?"

"My, my, brother dear, you are touchy tonight." She glanced over her shoulder to make certain her customers were still eating, then slid into the booth beside him. "I guess we're both nervous about our dates tomorrow night, huh?"

He hadn't told a soul! Not a soul! How the hell had his sister found out?

"Wipe the shocked look off your face. Miss Sophie told me."

"Who told her?"

Bridget shrugged. "Who knows? What difference does it make?"

"It makes a big difference to me. The whole town will be lined up outside the restaurant to see if I use the right fork!"

"You only get one," his sister teased. "This isn't exactly the Ritz."

"Okay. So I might use my fork instead of my knife to eat green peas."

"Broccoli is the special on Saturday night."

"Bridget!" he snapped, emphasizing the second syllable, a sure sign that he'd had enough of her tormenting.

"Come to think of it, let me give you some sisterly advice—order the mashed potatoes. You can always squish the peas into the potatoes. That's what everybody else does."

"Yuck!"

"Yuck?" Bridget giggled. Her brother never used any form of her favorite word. Her eyes dropped to the sack clenched in his hands. "What's in the sack?"

"Your tip. I'm thinking about returning it. How many people have you told about my taking Jennifer out for dinner?"

Bridget tapped her finger on her lip as though tabulating whom she'd told. "One . . ."

"Just one? Good."

"Maybe two . . ."

"That's two too many."

". . . dozen."

"Two dozen!" Duke slapped his forehead. "Why didn't you rent a billboard?"

"Sophie and I thought of that idea, but I'm short on cash, remember?"

"So help me, Bridget . . ."

A peal of giggles bubbled from behind her hand. "You're safe. I haven't told anybody."

"Good. It's bad enough having her turn me down at the last minute, without everybody in town knowing the mayor threw rotten eggs in my face."

The giggles abruptly ceased. "She broke the date?"

"Yeah, I'm fairly certain she did. There's a note along with my paycheck, but I haven't read it yet."

"What do you mean? Haven't you opened your paycheck?" She plucked it from his pocket and ripped off the corner. "Aren't you the one who tells me fear is worse than reality?" Her eyes skimmed the note, then merrily danced with contained mirth as she said, "It's worse than you thought."

"I'm fired, too?"

In a mock tone of gravity, she answered with a straight face, "Worse. Clementine lost your social security number. She'd appreciate your bringing it by the office Monday."

Duke grabbed the slip of pink paper from Bridget's hand and she grabbed the sack. "Lemme see."

While her brother read the note, Bridget opened the sack. Squealing with delight, she bounced on the seat cushion, unscrewed the bottle cap and inhaled.

"Obsession! Oh, Duke, it's so expensive. You shouldn't have...."

Rid of his own fear, he teased, "You're right. I ought to take it back and get a refund. Little stinkers don't need perfume."

"But you love little stinkers, don't you?" She spritzed her wrist, then brushed it across the dark stubble of his five o'clock shadow. "Now we're both stinkers."

She scooted from the booth when she saw her customer wave at her. As she rose to her feet she saw the mayor walking in their direction.

"Don't look now, but the mayor is coming down the street. She usually eats here on Friday night."

"Oh, yeah?" Torn between wanting to be with her and not wanting to give her the opportunity to break their date, he warily glanced through the window. Then, making a decision, he stood up.

Jennifer lengthened her stride as she walked in front of her brother's grocery store. She kept her eyes on the cracks in the sidewalk as though their long-deceased mother was in danger of having her back broken should she step on a crack.

On rare occasions, George invited her out to his house for dinner on Saturday night. I'd just have to tell him I have a previous engagement, she mused. And then he'd start prying information out of me like a miner who's had his first sniff of gold. He'd pick and pick and pick until I told him the truth, which would result in another quarrel, or a lie, which would make me feel like a coward.

She'd looked forward to this date; she wasn't going to let her stuffed-shirt brother ruin it for her. Tomorrow night the whole town would know. Sunday morning before church, George could arrive with the signed petitions asking for her resignation.

"Mayor McMann," Duke said, touching the brim of his hat respectfully. He'd decided discretion was the better part of valor. Actually, seeing her dressed for work in a light blue linen suit, all crisp and immaculate, made a formal greeting seem appropriate. Gone were the grubby faded jeans, cotton shirt and wind-blown hair that made her his Jenny. "Nice day."

"Duke, I was just thinking of you."

A warm breeze skirted between them. She stood close enough to smell his . . . after-shave? Obsession? Was that perfume he was wearing?

He increased the volume of his voice in case anyone was listening. To the casual observer he wanted to appear friendly and courteous but not too familiar. "I'm doing fine. The job is doing really well."

"Nice cologne you're wearing," she said, sniffing loudly. She brushed back her hair and pressed her finger to her hearing aid. Something was wrong with one of their ears. Hers worked perfectly. "Is something wrong with your hearing?"

"Nope. Everything's fine." He lowered his voice. "I'll explain about the perfume tomorrow. Can I still pick you up at six-thirty?"

"I'm glad to hear it," Jennifer replied loudly, matching his tone. It thoroughly griped her to be carrying on as though they were plotting a major felony in undertones while loudly passing the time of day. "Are you ashamed to be seen talking to me? Shall I meet you in a dark alley tomorrow night?"

Duke forced a laugh. "Very funny," he hissed under his breath. Louder, he added, "Have a nice weekend, Mayor. You can count on me to be back on the job, bright and early, Monday morning."

With the wink of an eye, he was gone and she was left gawking after him. Instinctively she knew he'd felt obligated to protect her reputation by acting like a congenial employee.

"What the heck are you going to do tomorrow night?" she muttered, clutching her purse under her arm. The corner of the book jabbed her in the armpit; she shoved it deeper into her purse. "Too bad it isn't Halloween. I could decorate a brown paper bag and wear it over my head so no one would recognize me!"

Sophie double-parked her car, honked and called, "Jennifer! Are you okay?"

"Yes. Why?"

"You looked like you were ready to spit nails. C'mon. Hop in and I'll buy you a chocolate milk shake. Nothing like ice cream to take your mind off your troubles."

"I just saw Duke heading toward Elm Street. Don't you have to get home?"

"The casserole is in the refrigerator. He knows how to put it in the microwave and nuke it." She reached over and unlocked the passenger door. "C'mon. It's Friday night. Live dangerously."

The sight of Sheriff Elmo's car rounding the corner helped Jennifer make up her mind. She hopped into Sophie's car.

"Have you noticed how the police protection has picked up in our neighborhood?" Sophie asked as she pulled back out into the street. "Big Jim is wearing ruts in Elm Street."

"I've noticed."

"So has Duke. Big Jim's obstructing Duke's chances of being accepted by casting suspicion on him. You're the mayor. Why don't you do something about it?"

"Big Jim is an elected official who has another year before he's up for reelection." Jennifer folded her arms across her chest and huddled against the door. "Shall I stuff the ballot box?"

"I'd like to stuff his pointed tin star where the sun doesn't shine," Sophie mumbled.

"What'd you say?" Jennifer decided there had to be a malfunction of her hearing aid.

"Nothing, dear. I was thinking aloud."

"Think louder, would you?"

"As mayor, you could verbally slap Big Jim on his wrists. Police harassment is illegal."

"You want me to call Big Jim on the carpet?" She chuckled at the ludicrous picture that would make. About as ridiculous as what would happen if he stopped her on her dirt bike and asked for a driver's license. In both situations she'd be dreadfully embarrassed.

"Your office isn't carpeted, but you've got the main idea."

"A vivid picture comes to mind, Sophie. I'm behind the desk, wiping my palms on my thighs. He's towering over me, pointing his unlit cigar in my face, reading me the riot act." She shot Sophie a rueful grin. "It isn't the picture you wanted to see, is it?"

"No, but—"

"C'mon, Sophie. You know I can't chastise Big Jim for doing his job any more than I can erase his memory."

Sophie parked her car and switched off the engine. Her bifocals slid to the flare of her nose as she unfastened her seat belt. Peering over them, she said, "So help me, Jennifer, he'd better quit calling me Soft

Soap Sophie every time he sees me or I'll do something worse than stand him in the corner!''

"Big Jim fussin' and fumin' just makes him look like a buffoon.'' Jennifer got out of Sophie's car and marched to the entrance. "Duke knows how to handle Big Jim... and the rest of the town, for that matter. He'd glad-handing them to death. It's difficult to be ugly to a person who's smiling and pumping your hand, isn't it?''

"I suppose so,'' Sophie replied, passing through the door Jennifer held open for her.

"I'll order,'' Jennifer offered, glancing around to find a place for them to sit. "There's one over there. You save us a booth. Chocolate milk shake?''

Sophie nodded.

While Jennifer stood in line, she wondered if Sophie's only concern was the sheriff's attitude. A couple of days ago, when she'd mentioned to Sophie that she had a date with Duke, the older woman had been surprisingly quiet.

"Hiya, Mayor! Can I take your order?''

"Two chocolate milk shakes, please,'' Jennifer replied, smiling at the heavyset teenage boy who looked as though he belonged on a tractor instead of serving fast food. "How's your dad's winter wheat crop?''

"Fair to middlin'. Prices oughta be up 'cuz of the drought last year.''

Jennifer watched Keith cross to the milk shake machine and pull the lever. Thick, creamy ice cream filled the paper cup. Good crops selling for top prices would pump additional money into the town. "You planning on helping your dad out this summer with the crops?''

"Nah. The farm can't support the folks and me once I graduate." He shrugged as he placed the drinks on the tray. "I thought I'd try to find a civil service job in Springfield. I hate to leave, but there's no work available within driving distance of the farm."

"I'm working on getting some light industry to start up in our area."

"Oh, yeah?" His face brightened. "Maybe the old shoe factory building could be converted. That'd be great! Good luck, Mayor."

Jennifer mulled over the thought as she strode to the booth. The deserted factory had become a dilapidated landmark, a two-story brick building she walked past every day without really noticing. No Trespassing signs stating violators would be prosecuted were posted at each entrance forbidding entry. An eight-foot-high chain link fence with a locked padlock enforced the warnings.

Legally, did she have the right to inspect the premises?

No, but who'd stop her?

Tomorrow, she decided, she'd find an opening in the fence. She'd pry off the nailed boards over the doors with a crowbar and take a closer look.

Sophie took the tray as Jennifer scooted into the booth. "What are you grinning about?"

"Breaking down barriers. Going into forbidden places."

Glancing around, Sophie mouthed, "The walls have ears. We can't talk about your date here."

"I was thinking about the shoe factory." Her blue eyes lit up with laughter. "But you're right. Tomorrow I'll be breaking the posted and unposted rules, won't I?''

Sophie stuck her straws in her milk shake. "There's an old saying about angels going where others fear to tread. You couldn't pay me to go in that spooky old building."

"You don't believe those Halloween stories you've heard, do you?" She watched Sophie shiver. "C'mon. They're as phony as Big Jim's tales about Duke."

"Maybe." She slowly stirred her drink. "But you ought to be careful . . . in both cases."

"Oh, no, Sophie, not you, too!" Jennifer groaned. "I thought you had faith in him."

"I do."

"Then why the friendly warning?"

"I don't care about his past, Jennifer." From the pained expression on Sophie's face, Jennifer knew Sophie was choosing her words carefully to make certain she wouldn't be disloyal to Duke. "I do care about you and your future. I don't want to see you hurt. I want you to take a long, hard look before you leap beyond being his friend. Promise?"

If anyone else in town had given her such a warning, Jennifer would have silently scoffed and blithely nodded her head. But she knew Sophie had her best interest at heart. Sophie cared for both her and Duke.

"Did you wring the same promise out of Duke?" she wondered aloud.

"Yes."

Mildly exasperated, Jennifer felt her heart sink when she looked Sophie straight in the eye. "You gave him a love-is-blind-but-the-neighbors-ain't speech?

That's why he pretended we were just acquaintances when he saw me on the street?''

"I did mention that you'd stuck out your neck for him."

"And everybody is watching to see if I'm decapitated?"

Flustered, Sophie removed her glasses and massaged the two red marks at the bridge of her nose. "I sound like a meddling old fool. Are you furious with me?"

"No, Sophie, of course not. And I do promise to think about what you've said."

Very, very carefully, she made certain Sophie didn't wring any other promises from her.

Chapter Eight

Chicken," Jennifer muttered, watching the pickup trucks and cars as they slowly passed by, waving in response to the friendly greetings of her constituents. "Too chicken to go in there in broad daylight."

Saturday was Lumberton's busiest day. People from the surrounding area congregated in the square and along Main Street. Wives shopped; husbands jawboned; children played. And Jennifer procrastinated.

Breaking and entering private property was one thing, but doing it in front of the whole county was another. She'd have to postpone her investigation until tomorrow morning, when the streets would be empty during Sunday school. Sighing, she headed back toward Elm Street.

"Hey, sis! You busy?" George shouted in a voice that boomed across two city blocks. "How about helping out at the store?"

"Where's Marge?" Her steps lacked their usual purposeful stride as she moseyed up the block toward him. She had avoided George this past week as skillfully as Duke had avoided her.

From the day Jennifer's father had died, George's wife had made it clear that Jennifer had "inherited" the mayorship and the McMann house; her husband had inherited the grocery business. On previous occasions when Jennifer had volunteered to help, Marge had politely but firmly declined the offer, saying that relatives shouldn't live in each other's pockets. Jennifer had caught the underlying message: All Others Pay Cash was meant for her, too.

"She's feeling poorly. Hay fever season. There's a line at the checkout counters."

Helpful by nature, Jennifer picked up her pace. It did cross her mind that George had made a mistake when he didn't hire Duke; Duke could have filled in for Marge.

"Which lane do you want me to operate?"

"Number two. I'll get the cash drawer." George opened the door and followed her into the store. Her worst fear came into being when he said, "Marge fixed meat loaf for dinner tonight. She said to invite you over."

Jennifer injected a false note of regret in her voice, saying, "Thanks, but I've made plans for this evening."

Briskly moving to the cash register, she prayed George would let the subject drop. She should have saved her prayers for later, when she'd need them.

She'd been on her feet nonstop for several hours when the first lull in business occurred. George sidled up beside her and casually asked, "So your social agenda is booked for tonight, huh? Big date?"

"Dinner with a friend." She picked up a bottle of glass cleaner and began scrubbing the expensive scanner George had recently had installed. "These scanners sure save time."

"Yeah. They're worth every penny I paid for them. Listen, sis, you haven't been over in weeks. Marge won't mind if you bring your girlfriend along. She always fixes enough meat loaf to feed the U.S. Army."

Of course, she had implied it, but her brother's assumption that her dinner companion would be a woman still rankled. She was considering tossing the damp rag with which she was wiping the scanner in George's face and proudly telling him whom she was going out with when the door swished open. Her tongue stuck to the roof of her mouth.

Duke and Bridget entered the store.

George followed the direction of her eyes. "Keep an eye on them. I'll call Marge and tell her you're bringing a friend."

"No!"

She dropped the bottle of cleaner to grab her brother's sleeve, but he'd already turned and crossed to the manager's booth. From there he could overlook the entire store while he called Marge.

While George's back was turned and Bridget was struggling to separate two grocery carts, Duke grinned and shot Jennifer a lazy wink. Her heart fluttered; her hands followed suit. The white cloth she held waved like a flag of surrender.

Bold as sin, Duke strode toward her. He cocked his head to one side. "Want to sniff?"

"What?" The sight of his smoothly shaven jaw and the vulnerable vein pulsing at his throat wiped out the memory of his smelling as though he'd recently toured a perfume factory yesterday.

"My after-shave. It's a bit less feminine than the perfume Bridget sprayed on me yesterday." His dark eyes glittered with amusement. For the lady Sophie praised to the skies for having the best memory of any of her first-grade students, Jennifer was delightfully forgetful around him. "Old Spice."

Automatically, she leaned forward. The clean fragrance of soap blended nicely with the aroma of his after-shave. His closeness drove from her mind all thoughts of where they were and who was watching.

A muscle flexed along Duke's jaw as he caught the dirty look George hurled down from his perch, but he stood his ground. He deflected George's scowl with a wide grin. "How you doing, George? Beautiful day, huh?"

Glancing at the raised booth, Jennifer watched her brother's face turn as red as the radishes in the produce department.

Duke casually picked up a newspaper from the rack at the checkout counter and opened it. Over the serrated edges, his eyes remained focused on her.

"Old Georgie Porgie looks as though he's going to have a fit of apoplexy. Are you two squabbling over anything I should know about?"

He'd asked the question softly, with a hint of teasing in his voice, but she knew if she scratched the surface she'd find a core of solid dislike under the flimsy coating of good humor.

"He invited me to dinner."

"And?" He turned the page, giving the appearance to an onlooker of being more interested in the comic strips than the conversation. "What'd you tell him?"

"I told him I was having dinner with a friend."

His dark eyes searched her pale blue eyes for any flicker of shame. He saw none, only a hint of irritation.

"He assumed my friend was a female. He also assumed, by inviting my girlfriend to come with me, that his wife's meat loaf was too irresistible to refuse."

"A-S-S," Duke said, mimicking Bridget's cheerleader style of spelling everything, "U and M-E?" His finger pointed at Jennifer and tapped his shirtfront with his thumb.

Jennifer frowned. With George hovering overhead, this wasn't the time or place to tell Duke that his spelling was as indecipherable for her as the inch-high headline of the paper he held in his hands. Duke could have been holding the newspaper upside down and she wouldn't have known the difference.

Duke watched her eyes narrow and her hand move to the small device inside her ear. His attempt at making light of George's assumption had fallen flat. He'd expected her to at least groan at his old joke. Obviously, he silently deduced, this was no laughing matter to her.

Duke refolded the newspaper and stuck it under his arm. He reached into his pants pocket to pay for it. Old insecurities raised their ugly heads. She's changed her mind, he thought wretchedly. With her brother watching, she's realized she's too good to go out with the wild Jones kid. Make it easy on her. Tell her something has come up and you have to break the date.

"George always jumps to the wrong conclusions," Jennifer said quietly. She took the two quarters Duke held out to her. He'd held them long enough for the coins to have absorbed his body heat. It gave her the strength to say, "After you finish shopping, I'll straighten him out."

"Jenny, I don't want to cause you trouble. Sometimes I still feel like the cartoon character in the Peanuts comic strip." Her puzzled frown made him realize she didn't know which character he had in mind. "You know, the one who always has a swirl of dust around him and a dirty face."

She chuckled wryly. She'd watched the Peanuts specials on television and knew he meant Pig Pen.

Her eyes reluctantly moved from his lips to the starched tips of his collar, down the front of his ironed shirt. He was dressed casually, but there wasn't a smudge on his face or a wrinkle in his shirt. "You don't even faintly resemble Pig Pen." She tossed her head toward the booth. "I love George because he's my brother, but I don't always like him. Trouble is nothing new between the two of us."

"I do resemble Pig Pen, if you write the word 'trouble' on the puffs of dust behind his heels. As far as George is concerned, I'm a walking disaster looking for a place to happen.''

Her smile became genuine. The way the earth seemed to tremble beneath her feet whenever she saw him, she had to agree with her brother's opinion, for once in her lifetime.

"An earthquake, maybe? You do sort of shake things up around town.'' She braced her hands on the stainless steel counter, leaned forward and widened her grin. "Are you trying to get out of our dinner date?''

"No, but—''

"Good.'' She flicked her hair over her shoulder and added dryly, "I hate meat loaf.''

Hesitantly, Duke returned her smile. He'd given her an out and she'd refused to take it. His heart swelled; he felt ten feet tall with the strength of Samson.

"Duke,'' Bridget called from aisle three, "I can't read Miss Sophie's handwriting. Could you help me?''

"Miss Sophie writes like she's still teaching first grade—circles and sticks,'' Duke mused aloud, tracking the sound of his sister's voice as he turned his head. "Bridget must want me for some other reason.''

"She's in the cosmetics aisle.''

Duke groaned, "Red Hot Pink.''

"I beg your pardon?''

"Red Hot Pink. It's the color of a lipstick she's been searching for.''

His eyes quite naturally settled on Jenny's mouth. Only a bare trace of lipstick outlined the perfect bow of her lips. Kissable, he thought. Very, very kissable.

"Strawberry Pink,'' Jennifer murmured, wondering if he would kiss her tonight.

Shyly the tip of her tongue glazed over her bottom lip. Her eyes lowered to the center button of his shirt to keep him from reading her thoughts: she wanted his good-night kiss, desperately.

"Duke!" Bridget wailed, snapping his attention away from the imaginary taste of sweet strawberries coating his tongue.

"I'll be there."

Jennifer raised her chin. She put her own connotation to what he'd said. "I'll be ready and waiting."

Their eyes met, clung, darted away, then returned. There was no misreading the slow smoldering heat of his dark eyes. He wanted to kiss her. Reflexively, her head tilted slightly to one side as she completely forgot where she was and who was watching.

"Duke! Do you care if I buy a lipstick? It isn't Red Hot Pink, but it's pretty close."

"No."

His single syllable reply sounded hoarse and hollowed to his ears, as though coming from a long distance. Without realizing it, his shoulders inched forward; his hands covered Jennifer's. Somewhere back in the far reaches of his mind a voice was echoing "no," but he couldn't obey the command.

"*No*, I can't have it or *no*, you don't care?" Bridget rounded the end of the aisle, saw the moonstruck look on her brother's face and muttered, "Ooooops! Bad timing." She made a quick about-face.

"Out of the mouths of babes," Duke said softly, stepping backward until his shoulders touched the rack of candy.

He glanced up toward the manager's booth. George's eyes were bugging outward. Silently Duke cursed himself for dropping his guard in public. It would be difficult enough for Jenny to tell her brother of their date; he shouldn't have complicated her task.

With the warmth of his eyes no longer protecting her from the cold chill of reality, Jennifer felt a shiver run along her spine as Duke looked over her head. "He's up there gawking at us, isn't he?" she asked.

Duke nodded.

"I wish George would crawl into his king-sized safe and shut the door behind him," she mumbled, irked by her brother's protectiveness. "Bridget, an eighteen-year-old, has more freedom than I do."

Jennifer was frustrated from not receiving Duke's kiss and embarrassed by her brother's absurd attitude; fighting mad, she turned on her heel. She couldn't hear what George was saying into the mouthpiece of the phone he held, but she figured he was talking to Marge.

"Tell her I have a date ... with Duke," she called.

Duke straightened his shoulders, ready to defend Jenny's decision with his fists if need be. His eyes narrowed; his hips thrust forward aggressively. No one, George McMann included, would bully her around in his presence. He'd tried being polite and friendly with George. It hadn't bothered him to have his overtures rejected, but by all that was holy, he wasn't going to let George browbeat Jennifer.

Like a fish yanked from its secluded pond, George opened his mouth, closed it, then opened it again.

"I'd like your permission to date Jennifer, since you're her only living relative."

"You don't need his permission," Jennifer said under her breath, from the side of her mouth nearest

Duke. She didn't need Duke protecting her, either! "This isn't the nineteenth century!"

Duke acknowledged hearing what she'd said by barely nodding his head while sustaining eye contact with George.

"Jennifer does as she damned well pleases," George said, snidely verifying his sister's grumblings.

Jennifer jerked on the white apron strings tied around her waist and pulled the bib over her head. George's patronizing tone rankled. She lived with him long enough to know he considered her to lack good judgment. The one time he'd dared to actually call her stupid she'd exploded, flailing her fists at him while he laughed. The harder he had laughed the more frantic her swings had become. She had finally bloodied his nose with a lucky punch. Just the memory of being totally out of control was enough to make her face tingle with humiliation. He treated her like a village idiot directing city traffic!

"Right now," she asserted, forcing her hand to remain steady while draping the apron over the counter, "it *pleases* me to go home and get ready for my date." She turned toward Duke. "I'll be waiting for you."

Duke grinned. "In ambush?"

"I'm not angry with you, Duke." She stepped from behind the counter and directed her parting remark toward the booth. "If I could buy George for what he's worth, sell him for what he *thinks* he's worth and donate the difference to the town's coffers, I wouldn't have to worry about the city budget."

"I didn't call you a dumb blonde," George blustered.

"It's not what you say, it's how you say it," Duke injected. He extended his arm toward Jenny. "Bridget! C'mon. We're leaving."

"This is the only grocery store in town," Jennifer whispered. "Do you want me to ring up the items on Sophie's list?"

"I'd rather starve," he replied truthfully.

Bridget wheeled her cart to the checkout station. "But Duke, what about all this stuff?" she asked, pointing to the half-filled cart.

Duke reached into his pocket. Listening to Jennifer stand up to her brother was worth the price of admission. He tossed a five-dollar bill on the counter. "Take the lipstick. George won't mind returning the merchandise to the shelves."

Grinning, Jennifer nodded. There was nothing George hated worse than stocking shelves. "No, of course not. It's his favorite pastime."

"Is it?" Bridget asked skeptically, giving George a look that pronounced him absolutely weird-o.

Audacity replaced Jennifer's anger. Her blue eyes twinkled with mischief. She took Duke's arm and hooked her hand in the crook of Bridget's arm. Like the Three Musketeers, they strode arm in arm toward the door. "Yep. George comes to the store on holidays and takes stuff off, then puts it back on the shelves."

Both women giggled. Duke chuckled, but for different reasons.

Once they were outside, Bridget said, "I can almost see your brother on Christmas Eve, decorating the shelves while Marge puts the S-T-A-R on the T-R-E-E!"

Duke squeezed Jennifer's arm. "I'm surprised George didn't have a smart comeback."

"I'm not. He doesn't want me to tell what I did see one particular Thanksgiving. He swore me to secrecy and he was afraid I was mad enough to blab."

Bridget clapped her hands and bounced from foot to foot. "George has a secret? C'mon, Jennifer. Tell."

"Uh-uh."

"Pllleeeease!"

"No. I gave my word."

"We won't spread it around," Bridget wheedled. "Honest! Cross my heart. I promise. I'll never, never tell."

Jennifer's smile widened. The day she'd caught George with his first girlfriend, making out on the wide shelf that ran along the back wall of the store, she'd crossed her heart and promised to die before she'd reveal what she'd seen.

"Stop prying, Bridget," Duke scolded. "She isn't going to tell you. She may be mad as hell at her brother, but she's still loyal to him."

Jennifer appreciated his understanding of her conflicting emotions. She had to admit that she wanted George to suffer just a teeny bit for humiliating her in front of Duke, but she'd never intentionally hurt her brother by making him a laughingstock.

"I couldn't expect you to keep your vow of secrecy if I can't keep mine."

"Did he blackmail you to silence?" Bridget asked, reluctant to let loose of what could be a tasty bit of gossip. She jabbed Duke in the ribs with her elbow. "Remember how I used to blackmail you?"

"Never mind, Bridget." Duke had told Jenny enough horror stories about his past. He didn't need his sister embellishing them. "You don't have to shake the family skeletons."

"At least your past sins are skeletons you can hide in a closet," Jennifer commented, dropping her hand from Duke's arm. Her secret was a living, breathing, nightmare she had to deal with on a daily basis.

Bridget stopped. "*You* have secrets? C'mon, Mayor. I'm gullible, but not that gullible. Everybody in town knows you're P-E-R-F-E-C-T! You're the cheerleaders' idol. We all want to be exactly like you!"

"Don't," Jennifer succinctly advised, lengthening her stride. Burdened by the certainty that the good citizens of Lumberton would be shocked to their bone marrow if she revealed her secret, she sealed her lips into a straight line. Her brother's escapade was safely tucked away in the back of her mind.

"Oh, look, Duke!" Bridget pointed to the cluster of high-school kids gathered at the far corner of the square. "Can I hang around town for a while? I have plenty of time to get ready for the game tonight."

"What about the groceries?"

"Sophie doesn't need them today." She pulled the list from her purse and shoved it into her brother's hand. "Can't we drive over to Camdenton and get them tomorrow? Please!"

"Go ahead."

As Jennifer watched Bridget run lickety-split toward her friends, she said, "My pantry is well stocked. Sophie knows she's welcome to borrow anything she needs."

"Speaking of borrowing, Sophie said I could borrow her Buick tonight. What do you think about driving over to Springfield for dinner? I heard a new Japanese steak house there has waiters who do amazing knife tricks when they prepare the food."

Awareness of the exact amount of Duke's paycheck and her reluctance to go to a strange restaurant, she replied, "We don't have to go to a fancy restaurant. The Towne House is okay with me."

"No sense of adventure?" Duke teased, unwilling to sit in a booth and be ogled by the people parading down the street.

"I'm a homebody. I like the simple life. It's...safe."

Duke had difficulty believing the daredevil he'd seen riding her dirt bike was the same woman whose prime concern was safety. "That's why you've stayed in Lumberton?"

"Partially." She could evade the real reason, but she wouldn't lie.

"I noticed the book you've been reading. Haven't you read about Scarlett's Atlanta and wondered what it would be like to go there?"

"Atlanta has a mayor," Jennifer joked.

"City government is big business there. You'd find something."

Jennifer felt like laughing aloud. She had an inch-thick correspondence file tucked in the bottom drawer of her desk from days when Clementine had taken off work. What would real city administrators do if they found such a file in an employee's desk? They'd fire her quicker than she could say "Bye-bye, Atlanta, Georgia."

No, she couldn't leave Lumberton, but she wondered how long Duke would be staying.

"Are you considering going to Atlanta after Bridget graduates?"

"No. I guess I'm a small-town, Midwest kid at heart. There's something to be said for being able to walk down the street and know everybody by name." They turned down Elm Street as he steered her back to the original subject by adding, "But I do like living close enough to the bright lights to enjoy dining at a good restaurant."

"We're close enough to the resort area to do that." Dare she hope that he'd stay? He'd said his job was going fine. Was he content with it? Her heart quickened. "Are you considering staying here?"

"And do what? You hired me for temporary employment."

"Another job might turn up. Bill Lewis is considering retirement."

"The county tax collector?" An elected position, he mused, certain he could count on one hand the number of votes he'd get. "I'm unqualified for his job. Quite frankly, even if I was qualified, I'm too ambitious to while away my life waiting for someone to retire."

"All the 'doers' leave. There's hardly anyone our age living here," Jennifer conceded with a sigh. Her steps slowed as she approached the walk leading to the front porch of her house. Averse to ending their conversation on a sour note, she said, "I made a pitcher of lemonade. Would you like a glass?"

The same gentle breeze that swayed the wooden swing on the porch lifted strands of Jennifer's hair and capriciously tangled them in her eyelashes. A man used to taking advantage of small opportunities, Duke reached out and brushed the silver-gold threads back from her face. Several long hairs clung to his hand. He wound them around his finger, letting his thumb slide over their silky texture.

Women who'd invited him to their apartments in K.C. had offered him beer and pretzels. Jenny was old-fashioned, like the Victorian house with its gingerbread cornices. Unless of course she'd offered him lemonade rather than anything alcoholic because of his father's drinking problem.

Jennifer felt her hair unravel from his finger. His reverent touch coincided too closely to the illusion of her being too perfect to touch. She was human, flesh and blood, not a fragile porcelain doll.

"Actually, it isn't freshly squeezed, homemade lemonade," she said dryly, hoping to smash her porcelain doll image to smithereens. "I bought a can of frozen commercial lemonade—"

"And nuked it in the microwave," he concluded, grinning. "Sophie must have shared her recipes with you."

"Nope. Though she did give me a wok and a recipe book for Christmas." Her face brightened as she hinted, "I don't do knife tricks, but I can stir-fry."

"Wait a minute," Duke protested. Jennifer had taken his hand and was pulling him up the walk. "I asked you out for dinner."

"Don't quibble over details. Let's compromise. I'll furnish the raw ingredients and do the cooking. You can read the recipe and chop the veggies."

"You aren't going to take no for an answer, are you?"

She dashed up the wooden steps, turned and dared to give him a sexy wink. "I could try gentle persuasion."

His blood pressure rose five points.

"That won't be necessary. You win. You be the chef; I'll be the bottle washer."

"Uh-uh. We'll work side by side, as equals."

Chapter Nine

Big Jim just laid a strip of rubber as he peeled down Elm Street," Duke said, closing the screen door. "He must be on his way home for dinner."

As he turned, his eyes widened in surprise. He'd expected the decor of her home to reflect the quaint charm of the Victorian exterior: overstuffed furniture, ruffled curtains, carved swans. Instead, the entire room was a study of creamy textures, from the plush carpet beneath his feet, to the inviting European-styled leather sofas, to the pale string wallpaper. At the far end of the living room the fireplace and bookcases were painted off-white. Pastel watercolor paintings hung on the walls and over the mantel.

"Very modern, very pleasing to the eye," Duke praised. The house, like Jenny, was a unique blend of Victorian traditional and contemporary.

"I modernized the kitchen, too," Jennifer said, proud of her decorating skills. "The bathroom is next. I'm waiting on the marble vanity top. It's been on back order for months."

"You and half the contractors across the country," he commented, following her past the curved stairway leading to the second story and into the kitchen. "The entire nation has gone bathroom crazy. Marble tops, gold fixtures, hot tubs. The last apartment project I worked on had master baths larger than the kitchens."

Jennifer grinned. She opened the glass cabinet and removed two lime-green glasses, replicas of a popular crystal. Filling them with ice and lemonade, she gestured for Duke to have a seat in one of the upholstered dinette chairs centered in the bay window overlooking the back yard.

"I've considered knocking the wall out between my bedroom and the small bedroom next to it," she admitted. "Architecturally, I don't want to tamper with the appearance of the house from the curb, but I have altered the backside of the house by enlarging the windows. The trees and shrubs back there are like a green privacy wall. Don't you think a Jacuzzi tub with an arched stained-glass window directly over it would be attractive?"

"Beautiful," he murmured, watching her move about the kitchen, totally captivated by her grace. He laced his fingers together to keep from reaching out for her and drawing her into his lap as she placed the lemonade in front of him.

She sat down in the chair at right angles to him. Her skirt touched the crease of his slacks. For only an instant, their knees touched. "Sorry."

"My fault," Duke said, scooting back in the seat of his chair.

Lightly, she twirled the ice cube around the rim of her glass to defuse the effect of his touch. Bits of lemon pulp clung to her finger. Without intentionally being provocative, she licked the tip of her finger.

Silently Duke groaned as her tongue flicked from between her lips. He wanted to tell her to stop. She was driving him crazy. His fingers unlaced. He opened his mouth to speak. Before he realized his self-control had slipped to a dangerously low level, her wrist was circled by his fingers. Ever so slowly, he drew her finger to his mouth and laved it with his tongue.

It wasn't the kiss she'd yearned for while they'd been at the store, but it was enough to set her heart hammering in her chest. Images pulsed through her mind as her eyelashes lowered. Mentally, she pictured him touching far more than her hand. The rough texture of his palm would rasp against the sensitive skin at her nape of her neck as he lowered his lips to hers, a trail of heat following his other hand as his fingers traced the edge of her scoop-necked blouse. His knuckles would press into the valley between her breasts as he lazily unbuttoned the tiny pearl buttons covering her lazy bra.

"Sweet," he sighed, "and tart. Like you."

Her fingers curled around the base of his hand. She knew she was inviting trouble, but she drew her hand to the side of her face. His thumb moved from the curve of her chin to her earlobe. Her lips parted; she turned them to the palm of his hand.

He'd kissed her hand once before and told her to save the kiss for a lonely day. She'd die of embarrassment if he knew how many times she'd caught herself staring at her own palm. The imprint of his kiss, warm and vibrant, had stayed with her.

"Jenny...I think..." His jaw clenched at the torture she administered so softly, so sweetly, with each wee kiss she strung on his inner wrist. Hand-holding and light passionless kisses weren't enough for him. "I think—"

"We both think too much," she said, with a small shake of her head.

All she did was think of him, wondering where he was during the day, what he was doing at night, plagued by the fear of someone piercing through his tough exterior and injuring his sensitive inner core with sharp looks or spiteful barbs.

"Don't. Jenny...please."

Her tongue traced the blue vein in his wrist. "'Jenny, please do'? Or 'Jenny, please don't'?" she asked, smiling at his verbal reluctance when she felt his fingers sheathe the nape of her neck, drawing her closer rather than pushing her away. She could hear his pulse drumming, skipping beats. She raised her eyes, giving him an unrestricted view of the longing in them. "Kiss me, Duke, please."

"You don't know what you're asking," he said hoarsely, swallowing, gasping for breath to restore his sanity.

One peppermint candy cane, he thought, his eyes shutting as his mind slipped back into the past, away from the temptation of stealing one of her sweet kisses, to a small piece of red-and-white candy.

Should he take the risk? Would he be able to stop with one kiss? Or would he want more kisses, more peppermints? Would he pay the same price he'd paid for taking the candy? Would she exile him while the flavor of her kiss still coated his tongue?

"One kiss?"

He was a born risk taker, and he claimed her reverently with his kiss.

The minty flavor of her breath triggered his desire. His arm circled her waist; he agilely drew her onto his lap. Her arm twined around his shoulders as naturally as his tongue slipped inside her mouth. Her other hand pressed against his chest; his heart pounded irregularly beneath her palm. No woman had ever tasted so sweet to him.

Time was suspended. No past and no future marred their kiss.

She melted against him, warmed by the heat radiating through his shirt, through her blouse, until her skin felt aflame. His feverish kiss held an urgency that fulfilled her wishful daydreams. No one kissed like Duke Jones. With a shuddering groan, her hands whispered through his hair. Her breasts flattened against the muscular wall of his chest. She wanted to press closer and closer until he completely absorbed her.

Her firm buttocks squirming on his hard thigh snapped the bonds of restraint governing his control. His hand skimmed from her thigh, over her slender waist to her rib cage, then covered her full breast. Magically, her nipple grew taut beneath his hand. He swallowed the small sound coming from the back of her throat.

His imagination went wild as he visualized her naked in his arms.

His lips, teeth and tongue synchronized with the movements of his fingers. As his fingers closed over her burgeoning breast, his tongue teased the tip of her tongue.

He imagined teasing the swollen rosebud tip of her breast with his tongue.

He sipped the velvet wetness of her tongue.

And thought of suckling her breast, wanting to nourish his body with her sweetness.

He enticed her to explore him by darting between her lips, swirling, then retracting, encouraging her to follow. She did.

He was sucking her nipple deep into the fiery wetness of his mouth.

"Duke...Duke..." Jennifer felt an exquisite shaft of ecstasy race from her lips and breast straight to the core of her femininity. She'd bargained for a kiss to satisfy her curiosity. What would satisfy the achiness that had settled between her thighs? She didn't know, but she knew Duke did. "Oh, Duke..."

He blinked, once, then twice, brought back from fantasy to reality. His eyes followed the inviting curve of her neck and the way her breasts strained against the summer-weight fabric of her blouse. Her ragged breathing threatened to burst the pearl buttons from their buttonholes.

Seize every opportunity, his primitive instincts clamored, urging his fingers to lightly flick the buttonholes open.

The kindest of Fates made the decision for him. The pearl buttons gave way, exposing the curve of her breasts. She restlessly shifted in his embrace until his eyes could see the dusty-pink aureole of her nipple through a thin veil of lace.

Duke Jones wasn't a man able to ignore his instincts. He'd lived by them for too long to let reason bar him from anything he wanted. He wanted Jenny McMann more than anything in God's green creation. The muscles of his right forearm grew taut against her back; his left arm reached beneath her knees. "Upstairs?" he asked, rising to his feet with her in his arms.

Deep, dark, mysterious passion shimmered in his dilated pupils. She felt herself drowning in the heat of his passion, robbed of the will to do anything other than nod her head in submission. "First door on the left."

The stair treads creaked under their combined weight. She couldn't hear their protest. Nor did she listen to the protests common sense gave her.

Yes, she knew loving Duke could be a mistake. Yes, she knew he could break her heart by leaving town. And yes, she knew Duke would eventually leave.

But she loved him.

A woman was entitled to make mistakes. If loving Duke turned out to be the worst mistake of her life...she'd glory in it. She'd treasure it as though he'd given her a priceless treasure.

Duke bent at the waist, lowering her feet to the shaggy carpet on the floor of her bedroom. Sunshine gleaming through the front window struck the metallic brass headboard. Wordlessly, he crossed to the front windows and closed the blinds. The room instantly dimmed.

Give her a chance, his conscience demanded. Even a hunter gives his prey a head start.

"Undress."

If she could disrobe in front of him, he'd know that she wanted him, needed him as badly as he wanted and needed her. If she couldn't abandon her inhibitions, he'd know it was better to draw back.

"Undress me," Jenny countered. She sensed that the distance he'd put between them could be measured in more than feet and inches. His eyes still glowed with desire, but the curve of his sensuous lips that had played havoc with her mind had thinned into a straight line. "Please."

"Are you ashamed to undress in front of me?"

"A little, maybe."

His dark eyebrow arched toward his hairline, silently questioning her response.

"I'm not perfect," she said, reaching for the buttons of her blouse. He'd expect perfection. Physically, he was firm and sleek. She'd scrutinized her naked body in front of the mirror often enough to know she couldn't fulfill his expectations. Her breasts were smaller than she'd have liked, her waist too thick and her hips too rounded for the ideal figure. Her legs were long and shapely, but he'd have found her lacking long before she reached her one physical asset.

"To me, you are perfect," he reassured her, his voice growing rougher with each button she opened. He focused his eyes on the hazy outlines of the bouquet-splashed wallpaper behind her left shoulder to keep his eyes from scorching her tender flesh.

Fear, such as he'd never experienced, made his knees weaken. His reputation with women was inflated. Sure, he'd been with a few women, but no one like Jennifer. He'd mess this up, just as he'd bungled everything he'd ever done in Lumberton.

What the hell was he doing standing in the middle of Jennifer McMann's bedroom? She was fragile, dainty, delicate. By comparison, he felt primitive, crude, coarse. Once they were in bed, touching, she'd know how different they really were.

"Jennifer . . . stop." He turned on his heel, unable to watch as she pulled the shirttail of her opened blouse from the waistband of her slacks. "We can't do this. You'll hate me within the hour."

Tears of frustration and humiliation welled in her eyes. "Isn't that my line? The woman is supposed to say, 'You won't respect me in the morning.'"

"Don't be flip." He braced his arm on the wall and took a deep breath. "You know I'll worship you tomorrow, just like I've adored you for a thousand yesterdays."

Her pride melted with each tear slowly tracking unchecked down her face. With his back turned to her, she dared to whisper her innermost feelings. "Duke, I've fallen in love with you." Duke's knees went weak. He barely had the strength to support his weight in an upright position. "Love?"

"Yes."

He shook his head, unable to believe a woman like Jennifer could love him. "You're confusing love with sex. They aren't the same."

"I'm not confused." Her chin dropped to her chest. Salty tears streamed down the back of her throat. "You are. It's that damned halo effect."

"Halo effect?" he repeated, momentarily arrested.

"I saw a program about it on television. It's where people think you're better than you really are." She sank on the edge of the bed. She wanted to cover her head with the pillow and sleep for the next two or three centuries. By then the raging inferno of desire he'd ignited might dwindle down to flickering embers. "I can't blame you for not wanting me."

Duke heard the bed crack, turned and saw the tears of despondency trekking from the corners of her eyes. Disconcerted by her shedding even one tear over him and amazed by her being crazy enough to believe he didn't want her, he edged toward the bed.

"Are you nuts, woman? I've wanted you from the moment I first saw you in your brother's store. I looked up and there you were, fresh and innocent, with those wide blue eyes of yours watching me. You have no idea how I wished we were both strangers meeting for the first time . . . away from here. But you knew who I was . . . what I was. You ran out of there like my eyes had set your clothes on fire."

Jennifer stared at the ceiling; her fingers bunched the satin coverlet in her fists. "You made me feel . . . hot and bothered," she reluctantly admitted. "I ran away to keep from running toward you."

"I should have run. I can't let you get involved with me. I'll ruin everything for you."

"What about what *I* want? Doesn't it matter that I want to be involved with you?"

"Why?" He had to make her see what she was letting herself in for by openly associating with him. "Do you want Big Jim dogging your steps? Do you want your brother to think you've permanently lost your mind? Do you want everybody staring at you? Whispering behind your back?"

"I don't care who follows me or what anybody says."

"You will," he corrected her emphatically. "You'll hate it and you'll grow to hate me because I'm the reason for it. I know. I spent years hating my father because he was the one who caused people to talk about me! I couldn't live down his reputation no matter how hard I tried. How are you going to feel when your respectable friends stop calling you mayor and start calling you poor white trash?"

"I've been called worse."

"What?"

"Dumb blonde. Featherhead. Flake!" She pulled her feather pillow over her face to hide her shame. To protect his self-esteem she'd almost blurted out the awful truth about herself. "Believe it or not, I know how it feels to be ashamed of something you can't change regardless of how hard you try. Only I couldn't run away from it."

Her words were muffled by the pillow. Barely able to hear what she said, he reached out to pull the pillow off her head. He jerked his hand back as he heard, "Just go away, Duke. You don't want me or my love."

Go away, Duke, pounded like a hammer inside his head. Go away, Duke. Get the hell out of here!

He'd heard that throughout his childhood. Finally, she was making sense.

"Will you be okay?"

"No." She felt certain she'd die if he took one step toward the door.

"Jenny, for heaven's sake, I can't leave you sobbing into your pillow. C'mon, sweetheart. We'll go downstairs, fix dinner and forget this happened. Okay?"

"No."

"Can I do anything for you?"

"Yes."

"What?"

She tossed the pillow aside and held her open arms up to him, longing to show him what was in her heart. "Let me decide what's best for me."

Duke stepped backward. He knew that if his knees buckled and he found himself beside her on the bed, a team of mules wouldn't be able to get him off her bed. For her sake, he had come to his senses before it was too late. With time, she'd thank him for not taking advantage of her weak moment.

He stepped sideways until he felt the brass doorknob in his hand. Through tight lips he said, "I care for you, Jenny, very, very much. Your friendship is what makes each day here bearable. I shouldn't have kissed you. This is all my fault."

She heard his footsteps and pushed the pillow from her face. "You're leaving me?"

"I'm going to get you a washcloth for your eyes. I need a minute by myself to think this through. I promise I'll be back."

Light poured through the door as he opened it.

"What do I do?" she whispered, distraught. She swiped the tears from her eyes. For his sake she could wage war with the whole damned town, but how could she win when Duke was fighting her, too? "How do I make him believe that I love him, despite what other people say."

She heard his feet scuffing on the hardwood floor as he moved toward the antiquated bathroom. There had to be something she could do!

The answer she found was as old as time . . . as old as Eve. She began finishing what she'd started. Within scant seconds she was undressed and stretched out between the sheets.

Duke turned on the cold water faucet and splashed water on his face. His emotions were at a fevered pitch. Cold reason, that's what he needed. He had to convince Jenny he knew what was best for her. What kind of friend would he be if he let her be ostracized by the community because of him? He'd already caused trouble between Jennifer and her brother.

"Some friend I am," he grumbled, reaching to the right to grab a towel and a washcloth. He wiped his face, then dropped the small cloth into the sink. A trickle of water seeped from the bottom edge of the faucet. He quickly glanced around the tiled room. The sink had a hairline crack zigzagging from the overflow to the stopper. "Downstairs, you should've stuck to a safe topic like bathroom renovations."

He wrung the cloth until water no longer dripped from it. He'd given her his word that he'd return to her bedroom, but he felt the urge to sneak downstairs and completely vanish.

Run?

Yeah, you're good at that. You can spend the next decade wishing you'd had the guts to give loving Jenny a chance. She's willing to risk everything for you, but you're too damned scared to try because you know you'll fail her.

Fear of failure, he mused, wanting to kick his own behind for slipping back into thinking negatively. The odds against his being successful in Kansas City had been tipped in favor of his failing, but he'd beaten the odds. Through hard work and diligent saving, he'd beaten the odds. He had a healthy savings account and the respect of the contractors he'd worked for.

He glanced over his shoulder toward the bedroom and then back to the mirror.

She says she loves you. His heart strings tugged his lips into a small smile. She wants you.

Are you going to let fear of failure strangle her love?

You must have some sterling qualities or she wouldn't think she'd fallen in love with you.

Are you going to stand here, scared to death of failing her, or are you going to be a man and show her you're worthy of her love?

Duke squared his shoulders. He'd been truthful with her. He hadn't seduced her with false promises of a rosy future. He had to credit her with having the good sense to know what was best. He'd take whatever she offered; friends or lovers, the choice was hers to make.

Jennifer plumped the pillow on the opposite side of the bed when she heard his footfalls coming toward the bedroom. She'd made up her mind as to exactly what she'd say and do. She'd risk everything for his love. Duke Jones could walk out on her, but he'd be carrying her secret with him.

Chapter Ten

I lied to you," Duke blurted, after he'd barely crossed the threshold of Jennifer's bedroom. The wet washcloth dangling limply from his hands contrasted with the rigidity of his taut muscles. His eyes adjusted to the darkened room, where her clothing was strewn about like the boulders at the lake. "I love you."

His pronouncement robbed Jennifer of the speech she'd been silently rehearsing. A wide grin split her face. "You do?"

"Yes...but our loving each other won't be easy," he warned, giving her one final chance to kick him out of her life.

"Nothing worth having comes easily."

He nodded, dropping the cloth he held onto the crumpled blouse she'd recklessly thrown on the floor.

She sat up, the satin coverlet slipping fractionally from beneath her arms as she extended one hand toward him.

A wry smile lifted the corners of his mouth. The dimple that had intrigued her appeared deeper in the shadows. He removed his loafers and socks, settling on the side of the bed near the curve of her waist and kissing the back of her hand. "I shouldn't admit it, but I'm afraid..."

"I'm afraid of rushing you, too," she freely admitted, opening up to him, without fear of recriminations. Wasn't that part of loving? Being able to say anything without worrying about being chastised later? "I was afraid of undressing in front of you, afraid you'd find me undesirable."

"You are most desirable," he whispered against her palm, his lips and teeth tormenting it, showing her the folly of having such outrageous delusions. "You're kind, gentle. I'm neither."

You are both, Jennifer silently argued. But she knew he wouldn't believe her glib contradiction. Proof of his kindness, his goodness, had to be tangible. "Remember the last kiss you placed in my palm?"

"Mmm."

"You told me to save it for a lonely day." Her heart thundered in her chest when she recalled how often she'd opened her clenched fist and stared at her palm. "I've probably worn it out looking at it."

"You'll never be lonely again," he rashly promised. His dark eyes lifted until they met hers. The coverlet slipped another notch as she relaxed her shoulders against the pillows. He bent over her. His voice was thick with desire as he said, "I'll be here for you, as long as you want me."

Forever? She knew better than to ask.

A shudder of pleasure rippled through her when she felt the slippery satin covering her breast replaced by the rough texture of his hand. She considered his calluses to be small badges of merit verifying his willingness to work hard.

"That feels good," she whispered, arching her shoulder blades. She barely noticed that the coverlet had dropped to her waist. She touched his shirtfront, manipulating the buttons through their holes until she could feel the texture of his furred chest. A shallow breath hissed through her parted lips as he shed his shirt and lazily hauled her up against him. "Better."

She lay pliant in his arms as he lethargically pressed her breasts against his chest. She was a sensuous woman who had an affinity for textures, from her touch-me sweaters to her style of decorating her home. He wanted her to relish the feel of him, to notice the difference between the soft smoothness of her breasts and the hard roughness of his chest.

His lips moved to the curve of her neck seeking the vulnerable spot he'd first seen the day she'd bandaged his foot. He'd wanted to kiss it then; he would now. He lightly kissed and tongued a path directly below her ear.

Self-conscious about her hearing aid, for an instant Jennifer automatically froze. The small, flesh-colored device had been a source of joy and humiliation to her. She'd felt joy as a ten-year-old hearing a mockingbird's chirp; she'd felt humiliated knowing how much.

Should she stop him and remove it? Did he find it repulsive? Her cheeks flamed at the thought of being less than perfect for Duke. Her hand moved toward her ear. "My hearing aid..."

Attuned to her slightest movement, Duke felt her apprehension as the muscles along her spine grew rigid.

"It's okay, sweetheart." He wondered if her appreciation for how things felt was related to her hearing loss. "Feel my heart pounding against yours? See how my skin quivers beneath your hands. Open your mouth and taste the saltiness of my skin. They'll tell you how much I want you without your hearing a sound."

His hands stroked her back, alternating deep massaging strokes with a touch as soft and feathery as an ostrich plume. He teased and tormented her until she relaxed in his arms. All the while he slowly counted backward from fifty to curb his growing sense of urgency.

"Duke..."

She wanted to tell him how his compassion touched her soul, just as his loving hands physically caressed her, but her thoughts scattered. A low, hollow feeling drew her knees upward as he lowered her gently to her pillow. Instinctively, her knees clenched to ease the ache.

He stretched out sideways on the bed next to her and spread her silken tresses across her satin pillow until a golden halo of hair circled her face. "Your hair is so beautiful," he whispered soundlessly, letting her read his lips. "I've daydreamed of doing this."

"I've fantasized about you, too," she confided. Her fingers splayed through the downy softness of his dark hair. "At the lake, when you surfaced from the water, I remember thinking your hair reminded me of a black velvet night. The droplets glittered like brilliant diamonds."

His lips curved and lightly kissed her brow. "You were miffed because you thought I'd invaded your privacy, weren't you?"

"A little."

He deliberately tugged the hair beside her temples. "No half truths between us."

"A lot," she amended. "You had the audacity to do what I've only imagined doing."

"Skinny-dipping?"

"Mmm-hmm."

His eyes closed briefly, long enough to form a mental picture of her emerging from the lake. Her hair, wet and sleek, cascaded down her back. Water beaded on her shoulders, then rushed to the puckered tips of her breasts. Her eyes were lit with love as she smiled a special smile, just for him, and opened her arms to him.

Silently, he promised in the near future to make that dream a reality.

His fingers moved down her throat to the rounded fullness of her breast. He heard her sharp gasp as his thumb circled her nipple.

"Sensitive?"

"Mmm." Her toes curled toward the ball of her foot.

Expertly, his hands cupped the undersides of her breasts. Her finger slid to the short hairs at the nape of his neck as his head lowered until she felt his hot breath whisper across one, then the other, neglecting neither. His teeth nibbled, his lips caressed and his fingers kneaded them until her heels burrowed into the mattress and her fingers dug into his shoulders.

In a growing frenzy, she feverishly kissed the crown of his head. The coverlet became a barrier between them. She tried to push it aside, but Duke lay on top of it. While her legs churned to kick aside the covers, she held tightly to Duke's head. To end the delicious sensations his lips evoked would be unbearable.

Her bare legs rubbed against his pant leg. It seemed impossible to her that his clothing hadn't magically disappeared. Relying only on her sense of touch, she traced his leather belt around to the buckle. She tugged at the loose flap.

Duke groaned. He'd purposely kept the coverlet over her and his trousers firmly in place. The cloth padding between them was essential. Stripped, touching her from head to toe, he knew the iron grip he held on his self-control would shatter.

"Wait," he whispered. His hand covered hers; his thumb held the metal prong of his belt buckle in place.

Jennifer pulled harder on the strap. The prong stubbornly refused to release from the buckle. Jennifer grimaced, touching Duke's thumb and knowing the prong didn't have a mind of its own. She yanked harder. Her eyes dropped to his waist, then lifted in surprise to his face.

"It won't come undone with your thumb over it," she complained.

"Twenty-three," Duke whispered aloud. Her knuckles feathered across his navel. His eyes squeezed together more tightly. "Nineteen."

Was he counting backward? Jennifer wondered. But didn't twenty-two come after twenty-three?

She framed his face with her hands. "Eighteen."

"Twelve." The lashes of his eyes parted; he watched her lips curve into a lovely smile. He moved his hand to the curve of her waist. "Eleven."

His inability to concentrate on the sequential order of the numbers gave her immense pleasure.

"Zero?" She whispered her encouragement as she pulled the buckle open and slid the leather through the belt loops, dropping it on the floor she teased his zipper downward. The back of her hand touched the rigid bulge beneath his briefs. "Love me, Duke . . . without restraint."

Magic was slow compared to the ease and speed with which Duke shucked the remainder of his clothing and returned to her side. His fingers splayed across the cleft of her ribs, then across the hollow of her stomach to nestle in the dark blond curls at the apex of her thighs.

"You blow my mind, lady. I can't even think straight when I touch you."

"Good." The heel of his hand made an erotic circle; his fingers sought the source of her inner heat. She empathized with his mental quandary. He was driving her crazy with the exquisite torture of his lips and hands. She couldn't have counted from one to five if her life had depended on it.

She twisted closer, arching against him, dragging her leg against the outside of his thigh with agitated strokes until she felt him move over her.

He protected her from pregnancy with the same loving care as when he braced his arms to safeguard her from the total weight of his body. Love glowed from her eyes. She gloried at his initial infinitely slow thrust, knowing from the tightness of his jawline what his effort to please her cost him.

"Jenny-love," he murmured. His hands guided her hips in a circular, lifting motion. "Ah, Jenny-love..."

His broken phrases of passion led her on. He was telling her what he wanted, needed. In a frenzy of desire, she arched, plunged, rotated, until she reached the height of passion. Her fingers clutched his buttocks, staying at the exploding peak, savoring its height. A rush of warmth filled her as Duke shuddered, then sank against her murmuring incoherent words of praise.

He shifted to her side. His hands moved over her waist, navel and breasts. Tenderly, he stroked her until her breathing lost its raggedness and slowed to an even pace.

"You're perfect," he crooned. "Unbelievably perfect."

Her head shook from side to side on the pillow. "Say anything but that," she mildly protested. "Anything."

Duke grinned. Her fingers lightly explored the depth of his beguiling dimples. His dark eyes captured the minuscule amount of light in the room and appeared to glow with love. "You *are* perfect."

Completely satiated and feeling good about herself, she knew the time had come for complete honesty between them. What they'd shared gave her the strength to meet his eyes and whisper, "I'm not perfect. Perfect people can read. I can't. My whole reputation is based on a hoax."

Duke blinked in surprise. "You can't read?"

"Not one word. The application form you filled out? It's hidden in the bottom desk drawer in a file that's an inch thick. Those paperback books I perpetually carry in my purse? I watched the movies or saw the miniseries on television."

He flopped his head back on the pillow beside hers. He was baffled by her disclosure. How had she ever pulled it off? A million questions entered his mind.

Warily, she turned her head to the side and watched the changing expressions of his mobile face. His eyes widened with amazement; his lips tugged downward. Disgust, disappointment? she wondered. She reached down and pulled the sheet over her as though it would protect her from his revulsion. "Pretty awful, huh?"

"Pretty clever," he replied honestly. "How the hell have you gotten away with it all these years? Someone must know. What about your teachers?"

"You've heard Sophie talk about my phenomenal memory. I'd sit in the front row, where I could hear or read the teacher's lips, and I'd memorize every word the teacher mouthed."

"What about tests?"

"There weren't any until fifth grade. Everything was verbal. I guess the upper-grade teachers looked at my past grades and gave me a break. Good kids who sit quietly and never cause trouble get good grades.

Sophie was a caring, noticing teacher but a lot of others didn't care." She sighed, thoroughly ashamed of what she was about to admit. Her fingers clenched the sheet's hem up under her chin. "And...I had to cheat a lot."

He turned to his side and faced her. "Sophie doesn't know?"

"No."

"Why? She's your friend. She would have helped you." He paused when he saw her throat working anxiously. "You were too ashamed?" he guessed.

Jennifer nodded. "Mortified. I thought about asking for help after I got my hearing aid, but I lacked the courage. Can you imagine what the kids in class would have said if I'd been in the first-grade classroom with the little kids?"

They'd have laughed themselves silly, Duke thought, remembering how they'd made fun of him about his clothes.

"Remember what I told Bridget?" she asked. "A secret is only a secret when one person knows it. Tell one other person and it becomes grist for the gossip mill around here."

"But surely your family knew. What about your dad? George?"

"Dad felt too guilty about shouting at me for ten years. He thought I was ignoring him. Parent deaf— that's what he called it. You can imagine how chagrined he was when the hearing tests were put into his hands. My grades were okay so he must not have made the connection that I hadn't been able to hear my teachers, either. I told him right at the end."

"Even George doesn't know? Dammit, Jenny, you worked at the store until you were elected mayor. He has to know."

"He thinks I'm a dumb blonde." She grimaced, then shrugged. "He loves lording over me. I knew he wouldn't be of any help."

"But you stocked shelves at the store. How? You couldn't read the labels."

"Most canned goods have pictures on the labels. When I ran across a case that didn't, I stacked them to the side and told George that was his share of the work."

"What about operating the cash register?"

"Numbers are no problem. They look the same and sound the same. I've always been good at math. After graduation, I wanted to go to Mizzou and major in math, but I knew I'd flunk the entrance exams."

She edged closer until they were almost nose to nose, searching for signs of his disgust. His one eyebrow was raised with curiosity as he asked questions; his teeth worried his bottom lip with concern. There were no signs of his being repulsed by what she'd revealed.

"So you stayed in Lumberton."

"I couldn't leave. I tried; it didn't work. Here, everybody thinks..."

"You're perfect," Duke finished for her.

Small pieces of the puzzle that was Jennifer fell into place for Duke. She rode her dirt bike or walked to work because she didn't have a driver's license. Unable to read, she wouldn't be able to pass the written test. He recalled the blank look on Jennifer's face when Bridget spelled words. Unless the context gave clues as to what his sister spelled, Jennifer didn't have the vaguest notion as to what Bridget meant.

The way she avidly watched his lips had to be a carryover from the days when she couldn't hear clearly. It explained her self-consciousness about her hearing aid. When she was in a situation that demanded being able to read, she automatically touched her ear.

The clues had been there, but he'd missed them.

"What about being mayor? Doesn't a mayor have to be able to read?"

"Not if Clementine is the secretary. There are advantages to having a ditz in the front office. She thinks I have her tape-record the incoming mail because I'm too busy to read it. Since she can't type or take shorthand, I tape the replies to the letters and a friend of hers in another department types them. If something gets bungled, everybody knows how lackadaisical Clementine is and figures it's her fault."

"What do you do when she's sick?"

Jennifer frowned. "Those letters are in the file along with your application form. Most people call or stop me on the street if they've written a letter that I haven't responded to. I feel guilty as all get-out for not being able to perform my job properly, but what am I to do?"

"Get help." His fingers curved around the side of her neck. He didn't know the first thing about teaching someone how to read. "Let me talk to Sophie."

"Uh-uh. It's our secret."

"But, Jenny-love, I can't help you. I wouldn't know where to begin."

"But you can. Tomorrow, I could bring that file home and you could read it to me."

"That's only a temporary solution." He tugged on her earlobe. "Listen to me, Jenny, listen carefully. You are going to learn how to read. I'll borrow some teacher's manuals and primers from Sophie's bookshelves."

Groaning, Jennifer shook her head. Her voice mimicked the high-pitched tone of a child's voice as she recited, "See Dick run. Run, run, run. See the ball. See Dick chase the ball. Run, run, run, Dick!"

"You still remember them? Word for word?"

"I can recite the whole Dick and Jane series, plus most of the stories in the readers."

"There have to be other series. I'll find something you haven't memorized." As he spoke, he felt her hand slithering up his arm and over his shoulder to his nape. "Tactile memorization?"

"Mmm."

"That's the sound an *m* makes. It's the first letter in mmmine. Mmmodest." He tugged the sheet from under her chin. With his finger, he wrote the letter on her chest. "That's an *M*. Do you want mmmore?"

A slow smile formed on her lips. "Mmm. Marvelous. I've heard reading was fun. I think I could enjoy learning how to read with you as the teacher."

"Before the evening is over," he promised, "you're going to know the sounds of the whole alphabet."

"I hear you," she crooned with a happy lilt in her voice. Her forefinger trapped an *M* on his upper lip. "Let's continue with *m* as in mmmouth."

"And maybe." The surge of desire her slightest touch caused would be detrimental to her reading lesson. "Maybe we should continue these lessons downstairs, over dinner, with a table between us."

"Why?"

"If I can't count backward, I sure as heck can't get from *A* to *Z*."

Jennifer grinned just as the doorbell pealed its eight-toned melody.

Startled into action, Duke swung his legs off the side of the bed and pulled on his slacks.

"Who could that be?" Jennifer wondered aloud. "I'm not expecting company."

"George?" Duke mouthed soundlessly.

Slipping off her side of the bed, Jennifer strode to the closet, pulled her terry-cloth robe off the peg and crossed to the front window. "The store is still open." She peeked through the front blinds. Her eyes widened. "The sheriff's car is parked out front. You stay up here. I'll be right back."

The doorbell chimed again; the screen door slammed against its frame as the side of Big Jim's fist pounded against it.

"Hold on to your britches, Big Jim." She ran barefooted down the steps. "I'll be right there!"

"Everything okay in there?" the sheriff hollered before she crossed the entry hall.

Jennifer yanked the door open wide, sucking cigar smoke into her face. She pointed to the Thank You For Not Smoking sign above the doorbell button. "You're polluting my air, Big Jim. Other than that, everything is fine."

"I saw a suspicious character on your porch earlier."

She didn't have to guess whom. "Duke walked me home from the square."

"He pesterin' you?"

Amusement crinkled the corners of her eyes. "No."

"He still here?"

She settled her hand on her hip. Unwilling to tell a bold-faced lie and yet aware of how scantily she was clothed, she said, "You're being paged on your radio."

"I don't hear nothing." He turned toward his car. "I guess I'd better check in, though. You sure you don't have an unwanted guest?"

"Positive."

Duke Jones is on my Most Wanted list, she mused, openly grinning. It's a good thing the sheriff can't read my thoughts.

Big Jim scratched the back of his neck, which pushed his hat forward. "I didn't see Duke moseying on down to Sophie's house."

"You must have been circling the back side of the block."

"Just for your safety, maybe I should come in and check out your house."

Over my dead body! thought Jennifer. Aloud she said merely, "I'm going to have to check into the fuel costs of the police department."

"Patrolling deters crime." Surprised she'd dared to criticize him, he clenched his cigar betweeen his teeth and backed toward the steps.

"Sounds more like harassment than crime prevention."

"Oh, yeah?" His chin jutted forward pugnaciously when she nodded. He stepped off the porch. "Well, excuuuuuse me, Mayor."

"You're excused, Sheriff," she replied sweetly.

Obviously frustrated, he tossed his cigar into the azalea bushes lining the porch, then swung around and strode to his car. Jennifer stood rooted in her doorway until she heard him mutter, "She's growin' a sassy mouth. Must be from associating with an unruly incorrigible."

She took one step in reverse and slammed the door. "Unruly incorrigible!" she spat.

"Are you calling me?" Duke teased from the top of the steps.

"According to the sheriff I am. He may think I'm growing a sassy mouth, but at least I'm not getting too big for my britches! The only thing wider than his butt is his colossal nerve!"

"Ignore him," Duke suggested, buttoning his shirt and starting down the steps. But he was having difficulty following the advice himself. Big Jim was like a shadow stalking him, waiting for him to make one wrong move. If the sheriff had been certain Duke Jones was inside Jenny's house, Big Jim would've found some archaic law written in the law books and thrown him in the slammer.

He crossed to the phone while Jenny continued to fume. "I'm going to call Sophie. He'll be stopping there next."

"I'll get dressed," she murmured, silently cursing Big Jim for spoiling what had promised to be a lovely, lazy evening in bed with Duke.

He dialed Sophie's number as he watched Jenny climb the steps. Big Jim was a buffoon but he wasn't blind. Jenny's hair was tousled; her face bore the look of a woman who'd been thoroughly loved, recently.

The phone ringing purred in his ear.

"Hello?"

"Sophie, it's Duke. Sheriff Elmo is on his way to your house looking for me."

He heard her inhale sharply.

"You haven't done something bad, have you?"

"No." Quite the contrary, he added mentally, glancing at the landing overhead. "I just don't want him snooping around like he's on the tracks of a violent criminal about to commit mayhem."

"Where are you? Oops, I hear Big Jim coming up the steps. The doorbell is ringing."

"Don't wait up for me. I'll be home late."

"Okay, Milly," she gaily replied. "I'll see you at church tomorrow. Bye."

The line disconnected. Duke quickly deduced that her door must have been open and Big Jim could hear her.

Jenny leaned over the banister. "You're staying for dinner, aren't you?"

She bound down the steps and twirled around under his appreciative gaze. Her sky-blue silk jumpsuit accentuated her fair coloring and molded snugly to her feminine curves. Her hair hung loose on one side and was drawn up and held by a silk flower on the other.

"Someone has to read the recipe to you." His lopsided smile kept the gibe from carrying any sting. "Or my offer to take you to Camdenton for dinner is still open."

"I'd rather have you read the recipe out loud in the privacy of my own kitchen than have you read a ten-page menu in a public restaurant."

"I hadn't thought of that," he admitted, beginning to realize how her reading handicap affected things he took for granted. "What do you do when you haven't memorized the menu?"

"On a date?" She made a face that was a cross between a grin and a grimace. "I played the role of the submissive female and let the man choose for me."

"What if I'd insisted on liver and onions?" His eyes sparkled with mischief as he thought of other entrées she'd probably dislike. "Or raw oysters on the half shell?"

She sauntered up to him and looped her arm around his waist. With a provocative smile, she replied, "I'd hand-feed you my dinner. Onions and oysters are aphrodisiacs, aren't they?"

"You're a wicked woman, Jennifer McMann."

"Shh!" She nipped his neck playfully and teased, "I'm the one who's wonderful. You're the wicked one."

"I've reformed." With a rakish grin he smoothed the sleek silk over her buttocks and whispered, "You are wonderful, though."

"Say that after you've taught me how to read and maybe I'll believe it."

Chapter Eleven

Duke Jones is rocking this town back on its heels, Jennifer thought, scampering down the trail leading to the lake, chuckling aloud. He'd certainly shocked the members of the church congregation.

Reverend Walter's false teeth had almost fallen out of his mouth when Sophie, Duke and Bridget had marched up the church aisle pretty as you please and seated themselves in the front pew. His eyes had rolled upward as though at any moment he expected to see great bolts of lightning crash through the stained-glass windows.

Pious as a church deacon, Duke had studied the program, picked up a hymnal and leafed through it until he found the page of the opening hymn.

Dressed in his Sunday best—a conservative navy suit with gray pinstripes, a white shirt and a subdued striped tie—he could easily have been voted the most handsome man in Lumberton.

Like the other churchgoers, Jennifer had had great difficulty paying attention to the sermon. Her eyes constantly strayed to him, wanting him to turn around, to bless her with one of his smiles.

She noticed the shy smiles passing between Bridget and Chad Felton. At one point, she was fairly certain Mrs. Felton had pinched her son. She wondered if Chad received the punishment for not paying attention to the church sermon or for flirting with Bridget.

The final amen had been sung before her silent prayers were answered. Duke turned, winked and gave her a slow, sexy smile that had her heart singing, "Hallelujah!"

She'd left the sanctuary and was shaking Reverend Walter's hand when she heard Duke stammer, "Good m-m-morning, M-M-Mayor M-M-McMann."

Her heart had fluttered faster then than it pounded now from the exertion of running down the path. The people clustered around them must have mistakenly interpreted his stuttering as stemming from his being in awe of her, she decided when she surreptitiously glanced at them.

Jennifer knew better.

"Stinker!" she muttered, grinning. "He was reminding me of our reading lesson last night."

She picked her way through the boulders to the secluded spot where she'd first seen Duke skinny-dipping. Her eyes widened with pleasure as she saw Duke, wearing only a pair of navy swim trunks, stretched out on a flat rock, sunning himself.

"How'd you beat me here?" she asked, dropping down on her knees beside him.

Lazily, Duke opened one eye, admiring her red shorts and skimpy white top. The stripe of pale skin between her top and shorts made his mouth water. Wordlessly, he pointed to his lips.

More than happy to obey his silent command, Jennifer put the folder she'd been clutching to her chest on the stack of books he'd brought and bestowed his lips with a light kiss.

"Mmm. You don't happen to have a golden ball you'd like to toss into the lake, do you?" He stretched out his hand to reach for her folder. "This will do."

"Don't you dare!"

She slapped at his hand, but he managed to grab it and hold it over his head, out of her reach.

"Grrribbit," he mockingly chastised, giving his best frog imitation. "How am I going to get the beautiful princess to take me home and put me on her pillow unless I retrieve her belongings from the murky depths of the lake?"

"You're a frog and I'm a princess, right?"

His eyes shone brighter than the sunbeams reflecting on the calm lake's surface. "Right."

"Then as princess of this realm—" her arm made a wide sweep "—I command you to give me the folder, frog."

It suddenly dawned on Duke that she hadn't read the fairy tale. She didn't know the story line. True love was what had changed the frog into a prince.

"Kiss me, Jenny-love, and I'll change from a frog to a prince and we'll live happily ever after."

"Will I get warts?" she teased, lowering her mouth toward his lips. "Never mind, don't answer. I'll take my chances. After all, what are a few measly warts compared to having a happy ending?"

Her lips smiled as they met his.

He pulled her down until she stretched over him; his knees clamped against her thighs.

"Grrribbit," he groaned, when she ended the kiss too soon.

"Liar," she whispered, tormenting him by wiggling her hips. "You are changing. Don't deny it."

"Yeah," he chuckled, dropping her folder and clamping his hands on her backside. "From a frog into a horny toad!"

She rewarded his honesty with a quick peck.

"Reach over there and get the spiral-bound book."

"Now?" She feathered her finger across his lips. "I don't mind waiting a minute or two."

"Or maybe a day or two?"

She grinned her compliance, then added, "A couple of weeks wouldn't make any difference, would it?"

Duke pushed the enticing tendrils of hair that had fallen over her shoulder back behind her ears. "Procrastination? Why? What's going on in that pretty head of yours?"

"Last night, I told you I didn't know how to read because... because..."

"It proved you weren't too perfect for me to love?"

Jenny nodded; her face turned slightly pink. "You're going to think I'm stupid when you realize I can recite the alphabet and write the letters, but it's like copying Chinese. Meaningless. I don't know how to put the letters together to make a word. You're going to think I'm *really* dumb!"

"You aren't stupid or dumb!" he said, giving her shoulders a small shake. "Ignorant, maybe. Illiterate, definitely. But not dumb. Frankly, I'm amazed at how well you've coped. That took some brainpower and ingenuity."

She looked into his eyes to see if he was just being nice because he didn't want to hurt her feelings. His eyes steadily met hers. He'd promised her honesty, no half truths. From what she could see, he'd spoken what he believed to be true.

"But what if my hearing loss wasn't the sole reason behind my not learning how to read?" Her shoulders sagged. "I might be one of those people who have common sense but can't learn from a book."

"Sort of an Einstein in reverse? He could theorize, but he couldn't pour water out of a boot with the directions written on the heel."

"I'm worse off than he was." Her chin dropped; her shoulders sagged. "I wouldn't be able to read the directions."

"Look at me, Jenny-love." He lifted her chin with one bent finger. "I'm a high-school dropout. Last night I went to Sophie's and ransacked her bookshelves. At dawn, I was pouring over those books, confused and frustrated. I haven't been to church or prayed in years, but I was there today. I don't want to fail you . . . or myself."

She hadn't thought of it from his perspective. His success as a tutor depended on her learning how to read. Unless she gave an all-out effort, she'd be cheating him.

"I'll try," she whispered.

"That's my Jenny-love."

He wasn't mentally prepared for her squirming up the length of his body. With her knees on either side of his waist and the bird's-eye view he was getting of her breasts as she raised her arms, he knew he'd never make it past page one of the "Getting Ready" workbook.

"Do you have anything on underneath your top?" he demanded.

"Of course!"

"A bra?"

"Do I need one?"

"Hell, yes! With a safety pin holding the clasp together!"

"Sorry," she quipped, her tone not the least bit apologetic.

"No bra," he muttered between clenched teeth. His hands circled her bare waist and moved upward of their own accord. Temptation, thy name is Jenny, he silently scolded.

He closed his eyes and dropped his hands to the rough surface of the rock. Mentally he chanted his goal: teach her how to read. Again and again he mouthed it until he felt the surge of desire that was making his blood run hot begin to cool.

Unaware of the mental war going on beneath her, Jennifer pulled the thick workbook off the bottom of the stack and quickly ruffled through the pages. Letters and pictures? No words? She'd be old and gray before she could read the mail stashed in the folder!

"This isn't the book you wanted, is it?"

"Yeah," he said huskily as she shimmied back down, her cotton top pushed above her breasts.

"There aren't any words in it. This is going to take forever!" Still astride him, she moved from side to side as she removed her tennis shoes, then dangled the toes of her left foot in the lake. "We might as well go for a swim while we're still young enough to enjoy it."

"Seduction?" he asked dryly. His big toe pried off one shoe; he did the same with his other shoe. "Skinny-dipping? On Sunday? Shame on you."

Jennifer skittered her hands across the whorls of dark hair on his chest. "Can't you teach me without a book? For instance, sssss? What letter makes that sound?"

"*S*," he hissed, "as in sweetheart."

She lowered her torso until she barely brushed against his chest. There was only one word perfect for the feel of the light rasp of his chest hair on her breasts. "Sublime?"

"Super," he agreed.

"Salty?" She licked the hollow of his collarbone. "Sweet?"

"Stop! We've come full circle—back to seduction!"

She raised her shoulders and stared at him. "So?"

"We'll compromise."

He sat up, hugging her against him. The part of him the sun's rays hadn't touched was hotter than his bare skin. He shifted Jenny until they were both sitting with their legs knee-deep in water.

Jennifer braced her arms and leaned back on them. "Stern," she mockingly griped. "And stubborn, too."

"Smart aleck." Duke opened his workbook. The control he exerted over his libido resulted in a deep scowl etching his dimples into vertical slashes. He pointed to the rectangular strip at the top of the page. "The letter is in the box. The first picture is called the magic picture because the sound will be the golden key that helps you unlock words. Then there's a whole string of pictures. Trace the letter with your finger, then say the word the picture represents."

"You're determined to do these lessons, aren't you?"

She traced a capital *D* and a small *d* on his thigh.

He moved her finger to the page and focused his eyes on the capital letter; he dared not look at her or his determination would have waned into nothingness. "Yes. Work, then play."

"When's recess?"

"Jenny," he said in a warning tone.

"Love," she added, grinning as she saw goosebumps form on his leg where she'd touched him. "Jenny-love."

"You're lucky I don't believe in corporal punishment, Jenny-love. You deserve a sound spanking for flirting with the teacher!" He favored her with a sexy wink. "I believe in positive reinforcement—rewards. For each page you finish, you'll get a kiss."

Time passed unnoticed while she enthusiastically whizzed through page after page and sizzled through a variety of his kisses. Like the letters of the alphabet, no two kisses were the same.

Aided by her fantastic memory, her ability to hear and her desire to learn, she achieved what she'd feared was impossible: she was actually learning to read.

"We're going to put sounds together and make words," Duke said. "Make the *K* sound then add the *S* sound."

"Kssss." She repeated the letters, stringing them together. "Kiss!"

He loudly smacked her lips. "Now, *L* and *V*."

"Lllllvvvv." Her brow furrowed. "Love?"

"You're catching on!"

"*D* and *K* make Duke." She pointed to herself and sequentially repeated the consonant letters to spell I love Duke. Her smile beamed with pride.

"You're missing the vowels, but you've got the idea." Genuinely pleased with their progress, he set the workbook aside. A sense of satisfaction curved his mouth into a cocky smile. "We've earned a recess."

"No silver stars?" Hands at her waist, she arched her back to stretch the kinks out of her vertebrae. A pale full moon chased the sun across the cloudless sky. Wistfully, Jennifer asked, "Remember how Sophie used to glue tiny silver paper stars on kids' hands and faces before she sent them out to play?"

"Paper stars," he reflected, smiling, helping her to her feet and cuddling her close. "I worked harder for a paper star than I have for a weekly paycheck."

"I like your reward system, too." The tip of her tongue flicked over her lower lip. She could taste him. Her blue eyes hungrily glimpsed at his mouth. "Peppermint kisses."

Duke watched the dark centers of her eyes expand. His desire for her swelled. To assure himself of their privacy, he reluctantly lifted his eyes to swiftly scan the secluded cove. Sunbeams, the warm spring breeze and the clear waters of the lake were their only companions.

He felt no compulsion to drown the tranquil sounds of water kissing the shore, leaves rustling and winds whispering through the trees with the hoarse tones of his voice. He cradled his hand beneath Jenny's windblown hair at the nape of her neck and drew her against his bare chest. His eyes never left hers.

Make love with me, his heart beseeched with each accelerating beat.

Jennifer read his mind more easily than the workbook she'd labored over.

"Yes," she sighed, loving how the thick mat of chest hairs tickled her nose. She inhaled the smell of him. Sunshine, salt and soap—a heady fragrance. With one hand on his chest and the other at the hollow of his spine, her sensitive fingers relished the subtle tactile differences. "Yes."

His hold was gentle, but as her warm breath flowered over him it grew tighter. The urgency of the kiss he bestowed on her revealed how he'd held tightly to the reins of his passion as he'd rewarded her during her lesson.

As though by mutual consent, the kiss ended. Their eyes remained locked on each other. Jennifer raised her arms; Duke lifted the hem of her cropped top over her head. He hooked his thumbs in the elasticized waistband of her shorts; slowly kneeling, his palms caressed the flare of her hips, the backs of her legs, knees, calves and ankles, as he removed them.

Unsteady on her feet, Jennifer clutched his shoulder. She lifted one foot at a time; he tossed her clothes aside. She locked her knees to keep from tumbling into the water when he turned her around and leisurely kissed the sensitive crease behind her kneecaps. She had nothing to hold on to but herself; her arms crossed over her chest; her feet parted to steady her equilibrium. Even so, she would have lost her balance if Duke hadn't noticed her predicament, straightened and secured her in his arms. Still, her knees were in jeopardy of buckling beneath her.

"Your kisses make me weak," she whispered. He lifted her into his arms, and she willingly surrendered to his superior strength and agility. One arm circled his brawny shoulders. She needed his support.

Duke stepped off the flat rock onto the pebbled shore and waded into the lake. The chilly water had the same effect on him as the cold showers he'd taken the past week—none whatsoever. Waist-deep, he knew any fear he'd had that the water would render him impotent was absurd. But he felt Jennifer tremble in his arms.

"Water too cold?"

She looped her other arm around his neck. "I'm like a furnace on the inside. The water may start boiling around us."

He edged into the deeper water. He slowly lowered his arm, giving her a few moments to adjust to the change in temperature. She stood on her tiptoes. Her breasts bobbed against him; her hips rocked in the cradle of his thighs. Their legs tangled; hers polished, his muscular. Her hair spread on the water's surface, darkening to a honey blonde before submerging sleekly down her back.

"Shy?"

"You mean the swim trunks?" Duke asked with a chuckle. "Purely a precautionary measure."

Her fingers peeled down his waistband. "Why?"

"The male anatomy can be aversely affected by icy water," he answered with a straight face, but his eyes sparkled with suppressed mirth at her husky laugh. He finished the task she'd begun and tossed his trunks up on the shore. "What about females?"

She untangled her legs and circled them around his hips. Her buttocks clenched beneath his hands as she settled against him.

"Hot," he mouthed, answering his own question, then drowning it in a sigh of pure bliss.

Her sigh echoed the long hissing sound coming from between his lips. She felt his hands trail to her knees up outside of her thighs, pressing her closer, then retreating only to follow the same path. She bobbed in the water, floating and sinking with each caress of his powerful hands.

Skinny-dipping, she mused, fully aware of his eyes watching the rise and fall of her breasts. How decadent...how delightful! Somehow she felt certain it wouldn't have been nearly the same if she'd tried it on her own.

His mouth met hers with the passion he'd kept leashed during her reading lesson. While one arm staunchly embraced her around the waist, he intimately caressed her. Her kisses became frantic as her eyes squeezed closed and a million silver stars burst in the velvet darkness.

Duke surged within her; his hands guided her hips as he boldly thrust, long and deep, burying his hard male flesh into her womanly softness. Nothing had ever prepared him for the sensual impact of being tightly sheathed within the woman he loved while millions of minuscule air bubbles caressed every inch of his skin.

Suffocating in the sensual ecstasy, he sucked huge drafts of air into his lungs. Small, purring sounds coming from the back of her throat gave him the stamina he needed to keep their heads above water, to keep them from willingly drowning in euphoria.

Her name rasped through his lips as her heels dug into his buttocks. Her muscles quickened, contracting around him, causing an explosion that rocked him to his very soul.

Jennifer made no pretense of hiding the tears of wonderment filling her eyes. She framed his face with her hands. Drops of water had splashed, unnoticed, on his face; some trickled along his lean jaw, others clung to his eyelashes. She marveled aloud, "What have I done to deserve such sublime happiness?"

"You care," Duke replied a short while later, as they dried each other with the towels Duke supplied, then dressed. "That's different from liking or loving someone."

Not certain she understood exactly what he meant, she asked, "How?"

"Intangibles are difficult to explain." He buttoned the top button of his shirt and tucked the tail into his faded blue jeans. "But take that folder you brought, for example. You could have pitched the contents and no one would have been the wiser. Who'd know?"

"I'd know."

"Yeah, and knowing there might be something important in those letters bothers you. Why? Because there's something in here that will be of personal benefit to you?'' He saw her shake her head as he crossed to the object of their discussion and picked it up. He tapped the folder with his index finger. ''No, it's because there might, just might, be something in here that matters to someone else. Selflessness in the 'me first' generation—that's what your kind of caring is. Sublime happiness is your payback for caring about everybody, even when they don't deserve it.''

Unaccustomed to receiving sincere praise, Jennifer's cheeks turned rosy red. Her first impulse was to deny what he'd said. She quickly changed her mind when she saw the love in his eyes.

''Would you read those letters and tell me what's in them?''

''I'll go over them tonight,'' he readily agreed. ''The ones I think are important we'll go over together tomorrow evening.''

Chapter Twelve

After work Monday, Duke flipped through the pile of letters inside the folder he'd brought home. First, he scanned each page for letterheads of special interest to Jenny. The ones without printed letterheads were fit only to be filed in the trash can, but he read them with great interest.

The continuing Holtgrew-Gimble feud brought a grin to his face. The Hatfields and McCoys were rank amateurs compared to these ninety-year-olds, who lived next door to each other.

Bertha's letter complained of Phil Holtgrew's having the cussedness to burn leaves in his front yard. Smoke and soot had stained the birdhouses her "dearly departed husband" had built forty years ago. In her opinion, Phil was a "mean-spirited old coot" who got his jollies asphyxiating those "darling red-breasted robins." She hadn't seen one bird fly into her birdhouses since last fall.

Personally, Duke liked the smell of burning oak leaves. Bertha, obviously representing the birds, was going to "sue the pants off" Phil if he didn't climb up the poles and paint those houses. The last time Duke had seen Phil puttering in his front yard, the old man could barely walk, much less climb.

Duke noticed the date on Bertha's letter: January tenth. No wonder she hadn't seen any robins. They'd all flown south. He could hardly wait to hear how Jenny planned on mediating this problem.

Next in the pile was Phil's charge against Bertha. He blamed Bertha's tomcats for disturbing the peace. They yowled from dark to dawn on the picket fence surrounding his back yard. He wanted the same leash law that applied to his dogs put into effect for Bertha's cats. He hinted that it wouldn't be a bad idea for her to carry a leash in one hand and a "pooper scooper" in the other.

"Poor Jenny," he muttered, wondering how she would politely respond to those letters.

He continued glancing through the correspondence until he saw a letter typed on quality bond paper.

"International Shoe Company."

He skipped over the greeting to get straight to the body of the letter.

We appreciate your inquiry regarding the vacant building at 117 Main Street. With imports flooding the shoe market, ISC does not plan on reopening the Lumberton factory. We are aware of the dilapidated condition of the building. Should you or a realtor find a company interested in leasing or purchasing said building, please contact...

For a moment, Duke tried considering what American-based shoe companies might be interested. Unfamiliar with footwear manufacturers, he set the letter in a separate stack.

Two hours later, when the folder was nearly empty, he'd created an inch-thick complaint pile, a you-might-want-to-read-these brochure pile and a three-item definitely-respond stack.

"What have we here? Custom Marble Company." He skimmed the letter and reread it to make certain his eyes weren't deceiving him. Then he rolled across the bed to the telephone on the nightstand to call Jennifer.

He'd picked up the receiver and started to dial Jennifer's number when Bridget burst through his door, flung herself in the upholstered chair and sobbed as only a heartbroken eighteen-year-old can cry.

"I hate him! He's a low-down, stinking R-A-T!"

His sister's welfare took priority over making his call. In three giant strides he was kneeling beside her. "Who?"

"Chad Felton! That's who!" She hugged his neck, blubbering, "He's just like all the other jocks. He thinks cheerleader is a synonym for slut!" Her voice wailed to a higher pitch with each phrase spoken. "If you loved me, you'd drive out to his farm and clean his plow!"

"Shh, sweetheart. You know how precious you are to me. Calm down and tell me exactly what happened."

He patted her back to soothe her hurt feelings while his stomach twisted into a knot. Locker-room talk could be more malicious than a witch-hunt. Boys, trying to prove themselves macho men, could destroy a female's reputation by shooting off their big mouths.

He knew how it could hurt. Locker talk often crossed over to a hatchet job being done on other males, too. He could almost hear the jocks taunting him, calling him a sissy for not being man enough to go out on the football field. Never mind that he couldn't afford the price of the insurance policy required by the school. He couldn't remember the number of times he'd stalked off into the privacy of the woods, too big to cry, too hurt to contain the tears.

"Lisa said he put my phone number in the boys' john at school...and beside it...he wrote...he wrote...'Bridget watches submarines...call her for a good time.'" Her jagged gulping interfered with her relaying the story. She took the paper tissues her brother handed her and blew her nose. "I h-h-hate him! He can just go to the p-p-prom by himself! I wouldn't go to a dog fight with him!"

"Lisa told you what was written on the wall? What the hell was she doing in the boys' bathroom?"

"Oh, Duke," she snuffled, her exasperation flowing over to him. "Her boyfriend told her."

"Does watching submarines mean what it used to mean when I was in school?" Watching submarines was slang for parking on the winding lovers' lane that led to the old marble quarry.

Bridget shrugged and sniffled.

"Did you go there after your date Friday night?"

Her dark eyes squeezed tightly shut. Tears dribbled from her eyelids like a leaky faucet. "Yes...but we didn't do anything...much."

"How much is much?"

So help me, Duke silently vowed, if that boy touched my sister I'll wring his neck!

"Stop drilling me like a construction foreman. I said not much. Holding hands." Her chest heaved with a deep mournful sigh. "He kissed me a couple of times."

"On the first date?"

"C'mon, Duke," she wailed. "Even you aren't *that* old-fashioned."

"Where you're concerned, I'm not old-fashioned. I'm barbaric!"

The tone of his voice opened Bridget's eyes wide enough for Duke to see whites completely surrounding the iris. Her hand covered her mouth as she realized the possible consequences of having told her older brother what had happened. She tried to slip off the chair. Duke grabbed her shoulder and held her in place.

"I shouldn't have told you. You'll beat Chad up and Sheriff Elmo will throw you in jail." A fresh batch of tears hatched from the lump of fear wedged in her throat. "All the sheriff needs is an excuse!"

Duke eased the pressure on her arms. "Didn't you say you wanted me to go clean Chad's plow?" While he was at it, he wouldn't mind taking care of Big Jim's plow, either!

"Yes, but I didn't really mean it. But someone should..."

"Honey, I'm the only someone around here that gives a damn about the Joneses." His fingers curled into knuckle-white tight balls. He shoved them into his pockets. "Are you sure Chad Felton is the one who scribbled on the walls? You weren't the only kids necking out there Friday night, were you?"

"No."

"No, you're not sure it was Chad...or no, the road was packed like a parking lot?"

"No and no! Nobody actually saw who wrote it that I know of. And Chad and I weren't the only couple watching submarines. It's just not fair. I've been so careful to keep my reputation lily-white. There are other girls with goody-two-shoes reputations who should have their mail delivered there!"

"So anybody who recognized the Felton pickup truck could have written it."

Reluctant to let go of her anger, Bridget whispered, "I guess."

"Did you ask him?"

"No. I...uh..."

"Bridg-et!" He strung her name into two sustained syllables.

"I made a scene at the burger doodle, I guess." Her bottom lip trembled; she caught it between her front teeth. "I didn't give him a chance to deny doing it. I was so hurt and mad I just slapped his face and ran off."

It was Duke's turn to sigh and shake his head. "Honey, you didn't give him a chance."

"He has to be the one. Why would anybody else do that?"

Duke ran his fingers through his hair as he considered possible reasons. He should have known things were going too smoothly. Bridget was paying the price for his being hired in the maintenance department. It wasn't too farfetched to imagine Big Jim being in back of the smear campaign. He couldn't legally run the Joneses out of town, but he could make life on Elm Street damned miserable.

Big Jim wasn't the only person who came to mind. Other than Jenny, Sophie and Clementine, his turn-the-other-cheek policy had been met with raised eyebrows. Wishful thinking was the only excuse he had for deluding himself into believing his last name and his past reputation had been forgotten by the majority of people in Lumberton.

He wasn't a kid, like Bridget. He should have known better. Filth splatters the innocent as easily as it splatters the guilty.

"What do you want me to do, Bridget?" he asked solemnly. "Pack up your belongings and leave town? You can finish the year and graduate from a high school in Kansas City."

"No! I'll quit first."

"Do you want me to talk to Chad?"

The telephone began to ring. Duke strode across the room and answered it. "Clarmont residence. Duke speaking." He could hear someone breathing into the mouthpiece. That's exactly what he didn't need—obscene phone calls. "Coward!"

The receiver was inches from its cradle when he heard Chad shout, "Don't hang up! I need to speak to Bridget. Please!"

Duke covered the mouthpiece and called to Bridget. "It's for you. It's Chad. Do you want me to talk to him?"

Bridget ran to her room, calling over her shoulder, "No! I'm going to be the one who asks him if he's the phantom writer!"

Teenagers, Duke silently groaned, waiting until he heard his sister's voice on the extension and then hanging up his receiver. She'd be on the phone for hours.

Duke shuffled Jennifer's papers back together. He placed the two important letters on top and put them in the folder. With Bridget's problem temporarily on hold, he wanted to see Jenny.

Should he risk going to her house before dark? God only knew what had been scrawled on the bathroom walls at city hall. He moved to the front window. The sheriff's black-and-white car was parked across the street. Cigar smoke billowed through the driver's open window.

No hurry, Big Jim. I can outwait you. One thing I can count on—you won't miss a meal to maintain law and order on Elm Street.

Duke began pacing the length of the room. With the same precision he used when he oversaw a job on a custom home, he began looking at the wild idea that had occurred to him from a practical viewpoint.

"How'd you like a couple of bananas shoved up your tailpipe, Big Jim?" Jennifer muttered as she leaned over the front porch railing and spotted his car. Willful damage of city property, Mayor? she chided silently. The city budget can't afford car repairs.

Impatiently, she strode to the front porch swing and sat down. She glared at the first-grade primers Duke had left with her. Why try to read them? she silently asked. She'd have the same rate of success with them as she'd had with the paperback book in her purse. The cockiness she'd felt at her office, when she closed her door, hustled over to her desk and tried to read the first page of her paperback novel, had been knocked out of her.

After struggling to no avail for thirty minutes, she wondered how making words from letters had been so easy yesterday, with Duke, and so damned difficult on her own.

But she was determined to learn how to read; she wouldn't concede defeat. She'd repeated Duke's two magic keys. Sound out the letters and connect them. Then think of a word that would make sense there. Easier said than done, she swiftly realized.

Only the minute hand on the clock had moved more slowly than her flagging attempt to read Margaret Mitchell's prose. A first-grader could have done better. Hard as she tried, none of the printed symbols translated into meaningful sentences.

Frustrated by the mumbo-jumbo sounds coming from her mouth, she'd thrown the book across her office and stared out the window. Her self-doubts had resurfaced.

Before she was born, she must have been hard of hearing when she stood in line at the baby-making factory. When the genetic engineer had shouted,

"Brains," she must have thought he'd said "Trains," and refused his offer. When he'd yelled "Read," she'd heard "Weed" and shaken her empty head. Then, when he'd bellowed, "Dumb," she must have thought he'd said, "Gum," and asked for more than her fair share!

"Dumb, dumb, dumb," she mumbled now, disgruntled with herself. "Everybody in town can read! Everybody but Jennifer McMann!"

She straightened her legs, edged the seat of the glider backward and raised her feet. The chain connecting the bench seat to the ceiling of the porch groaned in protest. One of the primers slid off the swing's seat. Jennifer skidded her rubber-soled tennis shoes across the floor until the swaying motion stopped. She bent over and picked up the thin book.

Duke would know she was a dim-witted moron if she couldn't read this baby book.

She opened the cover, cursing the day she'd told him her secret. She couldn't fake it, the way she had in the Roadrunners' reading group. She stared at the picture of a freckled, floppy-eared cocker spaniel. Her eyes dropped to the large printed letters. Before she realized what she was doing, she mouthed the *s*, *p* and *t* sounds.

"Spot?" The dog's name? That makes sense. The story is about the dog.

Her eyes moved to the next page where she saw a young boy tossing a ball in the air. "Jjjj-mmmm."

A page later, she read, "cmm hr, Spt. Gt..." She couldn't figure out the next word until she read, "bll." Suddenly she knew it. "Come here, Spot. Get the ball!'' Grinning triumphantly, her eyes flashed over the words she'd read.

With the taste of success in her mouth, she flipped to the next page.

Half an hour later, as the sun slowly dipped below the houses on the opposite side of the street, she finished the last page of the first primer and eagerly grabbed for another one.

Engrossed in reading, she became oblivious to everything around her. The sheriff starting his car went unnoticed. The ringing of the telephone was a minor annoyance she ignored. Duke's footsteps whispering through her grassy yard and thudding on the porch steps also went begging for her attention.

In the fading light, Duke would have completely missed seeing her sitting in the swing hunched over a book if he hadn't heard her sounding out the words. He unlatched the screen door and flipped on the porch light.

Startled, Jennifer's head jerked up. A warm welcoming smile curved her mouth. Dressed in loden-green slacks and a mint-green shirt, he was a sight for sore eyes. ''Hi, Duke!''

''Hi, beautiful. How's the reading coming along?''

''Better. I finished my homework.'' She scooted to one side of the swing, tucked the fullness of her pink shirtwaist dress under her leg and patted the wooden slats. Steadying the swing by bracing her legs, she asked, ''How'd you do with your reading assignment? Did I miss anything important?''

''An exciting chapter in the Holtgrew-Gimble feud.''

He eased himself onto the swing and draped his arm across her shoulders. She snuggled against him as though they were one of the old married couples who regularly spent the evening on the front porch enjoying the night air.

Duke slouched lower in the swing. Buford holly bushes along the front of the house hid them from sight. The episode with his sister was fresh in his mind; he had to protect Jennifer from a similar situation.

"Dad said Bertha jilted Phil fifty years ago," she murmured absentmindedly, wishing Duke would kiss her.

Her finger traced the knife-sharp crease of his trousers. His thigh muscle flexed, flattening the crease. A shiver of anticipation raced up her spine when his head drooped downward. He brushed his lips across her once, twice, thrice, then lingered until her mouth parted. He drew her tightly into his embrace and deepened the kiss.

"I have good news." His fingers wove through her hair until his fingertips touched her scalp.

"What?"

"One of the letters was from International Shoe. They want to lease their building."

"Hmm." What he was doing with those magical fingers of his was far more exciting than hearing about a deserted building. She slid her fingers over his smoothly shaven jaw. "I went there today."

"Your hair feels heavenly. Smells good, too," he whispered, stringing a row of kisses along her cheek.

She crooked her neck to one side, inviting his kisses. "I had to wash the spiderwebs out of it. That place is...ah, yes...spooky."

Duke nipped her earlobe. He had to tell her about the second letter before she thoroughly distracted him from telling her his idea.

"The marble quarry had been deeded over to the city."

Groaning, Jennifer shifted until one arm rested on his shoulder. "Terrific. Just what the city needs—a hole in the ground."

"Yeah." With her lips flirting against his mouth, he automatically agreed to anything she said. What he needed at the moment was a wider swing. "I mean . . . we do need the quarry."

She skated the tip of her tongue over his bottom lip. His sensuous response gave new meaning to lipreading. "What for?" she asked huskily.

"Vanity."

Preoccupied with giving him mind-boggling kisses, she excused his lapse in coherency.

The swing rocked precariously.

Jennifer bolted upright; the forward motion ceased when her feet landed on the porch. "Does vanity goeth before or after the fall?"

"I don't know about my vanity, but we just shattered the mental image I had of old married folks swinging on their front porches." He blew a gusty breath between his teeth and chuckled dryly. Lacing their fingers together, he brushed a kiss across the back of her hand and said, "Something tells me I'll be eons older than Phil before my desire to make love to you wanes."

"Could I get that in writing?"

"Yes, ma'am." He glanced at his watch, then toward the street. "We'd better go inside and pull the drapes. The sheriff has eaten supper by now."

Leisurely, she gathered up her books while Duke retrieved his packet of letters. He took her hand and they walked indoors. She snapped on the lights while Duke pulled the drapes closed.

"You would have loved to have been at the coffee klatch this morning. Milly teased Big Jim about staying awake during the Sunday church service. Sophie scolded him for trampling through her daffodils last night. And I asked him when he planned on repairing the knuckle marks he left on my screen door."

"Bad day for Big Jim? Pardon me if I don't sympathize." He held the folder out for her to take. "About these two letters and my idea . . ."

"What idea?"

"The one we talked about on the porch—forming a company to manufacture marble vanity tops."

"Whoa!" She reached up and patted the side of his face. "You'll have to excuse me for not paying attention. I had other things on my mind. C'mon into the kitchen. I'll fix some iced tea and you can fill me in on the details."

He pulled the letters from his pocket and began reading aloud. Just as Jennifer spooned sugar into her tea, he finished with the letter from the previous owners of the marble quarry. He waved the two sheets of paper under her nose.

"Don't you see, Jenny? The newspapers are filled with reports on fixture shortages. Yours is back ordered. With a minimal amount of capital, we can lease the equipment we'll need to crush the marble and we'll only have to pay cash for the concrete mix, the pigments and the vanity top molds. Labor is no problem. We'll put flyers in mailboxes telling folks to contact members of their families who have scattered hither and yon. This could be the solution to Lumberton's employment problem." He realized he'd probably left a few details dangling, but he wanted to give her an overall picture. "What do you think?"

She'd listened intently. The eagerness in his voice made her dread being the one who had to shoot holes in his proposal. "What about excavating and hauling the marble chips?"

"For starters we'll pick and shovel the rock. There isn't a shortage of trucks around here. In fact, the town is overrun with pickup trucks! We can make do with them until the company can afford to buy dump trucks."

"All right. Let's suppose you can solve the transportation problem. How much do you know about marble? Aren't these grades...technical information neither of us knows anything about?"

"There are all the men who used to work in the quarry." His eyes dropped to the pastel-checkered tablecloth. His own father knew one hell of a lot about marble. Jebediah had been a foreman in the quarry when Duke was a tiny child.

"Most of them have retired."

"I'll wager most of them were forced into retirement when the quarry shut down. They've been living hand-to-mouth, eking out a living on small farms. Or they've been sitting on their duffs collecting welfare checks while they listened to the grass grow through the sidewalk cracks in Lumberton. They'll welcome an opportunity to earn shares in the company by working as advisers.''

"Apparently you've given this some serious thought."

Duke squeezed her hands in response. "Enough to know I'm willing to risk my savings on this venture. But there's one stipulation. I want every man and woman in Lumberton to be encouraged to invest, and every investor should be given a voice, no matter how little money they've put up."

"You've worked in the construction industry. You'll have to organize the project. I'll call a city council meeting and you can—"

"No, Jenny. I can't." He reached across the table and folded his hands over hers. "Not me. You'll have to be the wheeler-dealer."

Her jaw dropped in amazement. "Me? It's your brainchild—your idea. What do I know about making marble vanities? Nothing! I can't handle it. You're talking correspondence, contracts, lease agreements." She shook her head at the prospect of having to read page after page of printed material. "No way. I tried to read *Gone with the Wind* today and got stuck on the second paragraph. I can't . . ."

"Clementine's father. He's a lawyer. Appoint him to wade through the legal papers. Bring the daily correspondence home and I'll go over it with you."

"But, Duke, that's not fair!"

"Fair?" Duke dropped her hands, pushed back his chair and strode to the kitchen sink. "You sound like Bridget. What's fairness got to do with this?" Of all people, he knew it didn't matter how much knowledge or integrity he had. If you grew up smelling like trash, you never got rid of the stink.

"Everything."

"Why? Nothing else is fair around here. Do you honestly believe the community is going to invest their time, their vehicles and their hard-earned money in a company funded by Jebediah Jones's kid?"

"Yes, I do," she replied unequivocally. "They're coming around."

"C'mon, Jenny-love, they've seen that old musical about the shyster who came to town to sell non-existent band instruments. They'll think you're the librarian and I'm the guy teaching their kids to play imaginary trombones."

"I'll back you." She moved behind him and wrapped her arms around his waist. "This house is free and clear. I think Dad would have wanted to take any risk necessary to get Lumberton's economy moving forward. Once the community knows..."

"Stop it!" He wheeled around, breaking away from her embrace. His eyes shone like polished onyx, hard and brittle. His fingers clamped around her upper arms. "This town hates me. Some jerk wrote filth on the school's bathroom walls about Bridget just to get at me. I won't have them throwing trash on your lawn, the way they did my..."

His voice broke, as did his hold on her. He'd said far more than he'd intended.

"Your mother's yard? Oh, Duke, why?"

Because they were narrow-minded morons, his heart screamed. She had had more dignity and tenderness in her little finger than those snobs had in their whole body. And she had been beautiful. The trash incident occurred long after she'd put up with years of sly innuendos and crass remarks. Finally, they'd broken her spirit. Like a whipped dog, she'd disappeared, never to be seen or heard from again.

"Never mind. It's ancient gossip best forgotten."

He cleared his throat; the wad of bitter outrage remained thick on his tongue. Some injustices a man never forgot.

"Don't shut me out, Duke," Jennifer pleaded, her eyes brimming with tears for him. "You can't bottle acid inside of you. It'll destroy you."

Fiercely, he pulled her into his arms and buried his face in the clean fragrance of her hair. She was too good, too kind, to understand. It was infuriating to be assigned to the bottom rung of the social ladder at birth and have his fingers stepped on when he tried to climb higher.

What difference did it make that he'd worked days and gone to school at nights to educate himself? Didn't it count that he'd sweated blood to start up his own company? Had anyone, other than Jenny and Sophie, asked or cared that he amounted to something?

Hell, no!

Why, then, was he enthralled with the idea of helping the very people who never missed a chance to kick him in the face? He had to be certifiably crazy to want to help them. He should be gloating over the decay of their petty little kingdom.

But he wasn't.

He had roots here. If Lumberton withered into nothingness, something inside of him would die, too. God help him, he wanted to live here.

"It's okay, Jenny-love," he said in a hushed voice, knowing he was finally coming to terms with the haunting voices from his past. "Your love neutralizes the acid. You make me strong...whole...born again."

For long moments, she held him to absorb the brunt of his pain. She'd been wrong to try to force him into stepping into the limelight, where critical fingers would point at him, ridicule him. Eight years before he had run from Lumberton, desperate for the privacy to lick his wounds. Even loving him with every fiber of her being didn't give her the right to shed light on those scars.

"We'll do it your way," she solemnly promised.

Chapter Thirteen

Clementine, you don't have any personal-leave days."

The sun had barely risen; it cast an iridescent pinkish glow across her satin coverlet. Blinking the sleep from her eyes, Jennifer tried to focus them on the red digital numbers of the clock on her dresser. She groaned aloud, pulled the coverlet over her head—phone and all—and asked, "What are you doing calling me at this hour of the morning?"

"I'm sick," Clementine wailed. "I got positively drenched yesterday while I was sticking flyers in every mailbox in the county."

"You don't sound sick."

Jennifer folded her pillow over her face. The smell of Duke's after-shave permeated the pillowcase. Last night, when they'd both been exhausted from poring over contracts and lease forms, he carried her to bed, undressed her and stretched out beside her. He'd held her...no more, just cradled her in his arms until she'd fallen asleep.

"I need a mental health day, Mayor."

"Mental health day?" Jennifer mumbled, eyes drifting closed, a smile of remembrance curling her lips.

"Yes, a mental health day. If I don't get a day off I'm going to go bonkers!"

"Not today." Jennifer yawned. "We've got a million and one things to do to get ready for the town meeting Saturday."

"Pooey on your old town meeting!"

Jennifer's eyes shot open as though her secretary had uttered a blaspheme. "Clementine, I'll see you...*at work...on time!*"

"No, you won't! You've been working my fingers to the bone for the past two weeks. I've got paper cuts and hangnails and my hair has black roots! I deserve a day off, with pay. If you won't give me a day off, I'll...I'll quit!"

"You can't quit. Your dad won't let you. He's behind this project one hundred percent."

"You're telling me." Clementine groaned her frustration. "He's enrolled me in a typing class!"

"Good. You won't have to impose on your friend to type my letters."

"It's a *night* class," Clementine hissed. "My social life will be ruined and it's gonna be all your fault. What's happened to you? You used to be such a nice boss. Now, it's do this and do that. Hurry, hurry, hurry. You don't even take time to have coffee in the morning. Why can't things be like they used to be?" she complained, with a whine in her voice.

Jennifer didn't feel the least bit guilty. The wheels of progress steadily grinding, pulling Lumberton into the twentieth century, were music to her ears.

"We're all changing, Clementine." Fully awake, she flipped back the covers and sat on the edge of the bed. "You're changing, too. Last month you'd have been sound asleep at this hour of the morning. But since we're both up early, we can get down to city hall before eight, huh?"

Clementine shrieked a protest.

"Bye-bye." She returned the phone to the hook and grinned, eager to face the challenges of the new day.

An invigorating shower later, Jennifer dressed and rushed down the stairs. Inside the kitchen, she simultaneously made coffee, poured dry cereal and milk into a bowl and read the daily agenda Duke had left for her on the kitchen table.

"Feed the grapevine."

Although reading was still a laborious chore, she easily recognized those words. She chuckled at their private joke. With her phone being on a party line, the telephone wires stretching around the town were similar to a grapevine. On a daily basis, she made business calls that fed everyone's ears with titillating tidbits of information that she wanted them to hear. The past couple of days there had been so many people listening in on the line that she'd almost had to shout to be heard by Chad's parents.

Each person she'd contacted had been thrilled to learn there was a chance Lumberton's economy would be swinging in high gear . . . soon! The gossipmongers were now spreading constructive rather than destructive news, she mused.

She worked down to the bottom of the list. "5:30-6:30 Duke. City hall. Work on speech." She folded the list and stuck it into her suit pocket. "Slowly but surely, he's coming around to the idea of the two of us being seen in public."

Whether their meetings were accidental or preplanned, he no longer pretended to be a city employee currying the favor of the town's mayor with polite pleasantries. Gradually, the people who crossed their paths had gone from raising their eyebrows, to nodding, to actually speaking to both of them.

She spooned a bite of cereal into her mouth, slowly chewing it as she thought.

George and Sheriff Elmo hadn't changed their mutual opinion of Duke. Her brother continued to give Duke the evil eye as he pushed his shopping cart through the store aisles. Elm Street remained Big Jim's favorite place to patrol.

Jerks!

She swallowed, shrugged her shoulders and took another bite. There were more important things for her to worry about than how those two acted. The finishing touches had to be put on Duke's plan before presenting it at the special town meeting she'd called.

Duke leaned over her shoulders, unintentionally diverting her attention from the brochures of fancy marble vanity tops he'd spread on her desk. His finger pointed to a freestanding, ivory-toned sink shaped like a scallop shell.

"The molds for that one and the two on the next page arrived at Sophie's yesterday. During my lunch hour, I hauled them out to the shed, mixed up a small batch of ingredients and made the first pour."

Dutifully, Jennifer glanced at the picture, then propped her head on her hand and marveled over Duke's profile. The sun had tanned his skin to a shade of deep mahogany. Tiny laugh wrinkles radiated from the corner of his eye. Her eyes traced the hint of whiskers that darkened the strong line of his jaw. His dimple played peekaboo with her as he spoke. Wide intelligent brow, straight nose, perfectly formed lips, she mused, which all together formed a marvelous face.

". . . the marble dust came from Georgia, so it isn't exactly the same as what we'll be getting from the quarry here, but I figured we ought to have a few samples on display at the meeting."

One glimpse at the dreamy expression on her face told him she hadn't heard half of what he'd been saying. He shifted to the edge of her desk and leaned against it.

"Am I boring you with too many details."

Mesmerized, her eyes remained on his face. Was a full frontal view more devastatingly handsome than his profile? She couldn't decide which she loved best.

He waved his hand in front of her glazed eyes.

Responding with complete candidness, she replied, "Actually, you're fascinating me."

"Oh, yeah?" His dark eyes gleamed with devilry as he held his hand to her. "Care to come closer and tell me about your fascination?"

She put her hand in his. He gave one agile pull and she was in his arms, where she wanted to be. His hands settled low on her hips; her hands trapped his face between them.

"You'll get bigheaded," she teased, tilting her lips up for a kiss.

Duke lovingly accommodated her silent request. Her lips parted, inviting more than a brief kiss.

The sound of footsteps in the hallway and the door leading into the reception area being opened made him abruptly end the kiss.

"Someone's out there," he explained, gently pushing her back into her chair. "Are you expecting anybody?"

"No. I told Clementine to lock up when she left."

She started to rise, but he motioned for her to stay seated. He was behind the inner office door when they both heard a hesitant rap.

"Who's there?" She tried to make her voice brisk; it sounded entirely too breathy to be coming from the mayor's office.

Duke put his finger to his mouth. The brass doorknob twisted and the door opened. Jennifer's eyes rounded in complete surprise.

It had been months since she'd seen Jebediah Jones, but there was no mistaking the family resemblance between the two men separated by the oak door. They were of equal height, and if Jebediah had only straightened his stooped shoulders his physique would have been as handsomely rugged as Duke's. From his dark, longish hair slicked back in place to the burning fire of his black eyes, there was no mistaking his identity.

Triggered by the shocked look on her face, Duke reached to pull the door open wider.

"Come in, Mr. Jones, please," Jennifer managed to say. Her joints had stiffened, making it impossible for her to get gracefully to her feet. Her arm felt like deadwood as she gestured toward Duke.

Jebediah's eyes followed the direction of her hand.

The door creaked as Duke slowly drew it toward himself.

"Son?"

"Father?"

One voice was as strained with emotion as the other; each man wondered what the other one was doing in the mayor's office. The air immediately thickened with hostility.

"I'll come back some other time," Jebediah said in a defeated tone, a fraction above a whisper.

Forced to rely on her lipreading skills, Jennifer felt overwhelmed by a sense of déjà vu—this had happened before. Only this time it was the father, not the son, who'd come to her for a job.

"No!" she blurted, quelling Duke from speaking by casting him a hard look. "Duke and I have almost finished our business. What can I do for you?"

Jebediah paused; his Adam's apple bobbed as he swallowed his pride. "I've been hearing rumors about the quarry opening. Is that just a pack of lies?"

Duke nodded his head; Jennifer shook hers.

Give him a chance, Jennifer's eyes pleaded.

He's had his chance...and failed! Thoroughly ashamed to have his father in the same room as Jennifer, Duke was tempted to bodily remove him. His nose twitched as he sniffed the air for alcohol fumes;

for once he detected only hair cream and mouthwash. The old coot isn't fooling me. I know he lives inside a whiskey bottle!

Jennifer could read Duke's thoughts as clearly as though he'd shouted them. "It's a possibility," she said to Jebediah. "Nothing is finalized."

"I used to work there before they shut down." Jebediah's chin lifted aggressively toward his son. "You wouldn't remember 'cuz you were no bigger than a tadpole, but I was the supervisor back then."

From tadpole to frog to prince, Jennifer mused, smiling at the lightning-fast thought.

"I thought, maybe—" Jebediah paused again "—I could be of help if the quarry is starting up production."

"You haven't worked in over twenty years," Duke said derisively, mortified that his father had the gall to try to pass himself off as qualified for employment.

"I reckon marble doesn't change too much in that length of time?" Jebediah reasoned. "A man may change. Rock doesn't."

"After two decades, a man doesn't change overnight, either," Duke retorted. "Fifteen minutes with a pick in your hand and you'd be facedown in marble chips."

Jennifer was appalled. Was this the same Duke who dealt so sensitively with his sister's problems? "Wait—"

"I'm fit." Jebediah straightened his shoulders; his trembling hand raked across his newly shaven jaw. "I can work."

"Wishful daydreaming and getting her job done are two different things." Duke hated the poison that seemed to be pumping through his veins, but he seemed unable to control it. "What happens the first time something goes wrong? Are you going to climb back inside your whiskey bottle and drown in self-pity?"

Duke saw his father flinch as though he'd been brutally slapped. He heard Jennifer inhale sharply.

"Don't let him trick you with his lies," he railed, stepping toward Jennifer. "He'll promise you anything you want to hear!" He wheeled sideways to address his father. "Right? Tell her how you broke every promise you made to my mother. To me. To Bridget. I spent hours whitewashing the filth off the walls at Bridget's school because she's having to live down your reputation. Go on, Father, tell Jennifer—"

"Hush, Duke." Jennifer's face blanched whiter than Jebediah's face.

"Tell her how you let people dump their trash in your front yard and you were too damned lazy to do anything about it. You wallowed in it!"

"Shut up, Duke!" Jennifer circled her desk and grabbed Duke by the arm. Through clenched teeth, she said, "Mr. Jones, you take a seat while your son and I have a word in the outer office."

Duke was bigger, stronger, than she was, but he didn't resist when she pushed him through the open door.

"How dare he come to you, waving his dirty linen in my face?" Duke muttered, watching Jebediah cross to the same straight-backed wooden chair Duke had sat in when he'd applied for a job. He grabbed Jennifer by the shoulders. "You go in there and tell him that he'd be the last person in the country we'd consider hiring!''

"No, I won't." Jennifer brushed his hand off her shoulders. She held her voice down, but her intensity made up for the lack of volume. "You're treating him the way everybody in town treated you."

"There's one difference. He earned their contempt. He pickled his brain in alcohol. Don't give him a job because you think you're doing me a favor."

Duke would have given his right arm for her not to have seen him blow up. Never in a million years could he have enough time to divulge all the slights he'd been subjected to because of his father. But he had to convince her that his father's being brought in on this would spoil every goal they'd worked toward.

"Be fair, Duke! He deserves a chance just like any other person in town."

"He's had his chances and blown them." Their eyes clashed. "Hire him and you've put the kiss of death on this project. There isn't a man in town who'll back you . . . myself included."

"Is that a threat?"

"Take it any way you see fit. I won't have people watching me because of him."

"Dammit, Duke, I need you!"

"Then your choice is easy. Go back in there and tell Jebediah Jones to hit the road."

Jennifer shook her head. "This isn't like you. Where's your compassion? Where's your empathy? Why can't you put yourself in his shoes?"

The last ounce of venom he'd bottled inside of him spewed forth. "He made my mother leave me. He drove her away."

"Duke," Jennifer said, reaching out to him.

Duke crossed to the window overlooking Main Street. He shoved his knotted fists into his trouser pockets. As he blindly stared through the window, his voice was infused with pain and self-loathing as he said, "Nobody knows this, not even Bridget, but I was outside the window when they had their last fight. I remember crouching down, covering my ears because I hated hearing them rant at each other. But I heard. Mom said we'd starve to death if he didn't get a job. Puffed up with pride, he told her he wasn't going to take a menial job, that he'd never get another good job if he did. She wanted to pack up, go somewhere else for him to find work. He adamantly refused on the grounds that we'd end up on welfare. People around here knew him. And then came the big promise—things will get better."

A harsh sound that faintly resembled a laugh parted his lips.

"The Big Lie Theory... tell a lie often enough and you'll convince other people it's the truth. Well, this time Mom didn't swallow it. She told him she'd pack up the two kids and leave."

Duke choked on the acidity in his mouth. He coughed. His voice dropped to a raspy level.

"Wily bastard that he is, he knew Bridget and I were what bonded Mom to him. He told her she wasn't taking his kids anywhere. She sure as hell couldn't support us. And then their voices dropped. I could only hear a sprinkling of words...love...marriage...whispered promises. I snuck off into the woods and bawled my eyes out. That's where she found me, down by the lake near the place where you and I met."

He lifted his head as though he could see beyond the horizon. "Brokenhearted, she told me she loved all of us. That Jebediah would realize once she was gone that love was more important than his damned pride. He'd get a job and she'd come home."

Jennifer folded her arms on the desktop and rested her forehead on them. "He never got a job—"

"She never came back. She vanished without a trace. I tried to locate her after I left Lumberton. I hired a detective. He couldn't find her, either. She's nowhere to be found."

When Jennifer lifted her head long moments later, Duke had turned toward her. His dark eyes were devoid of hostility; they appeared flat, dead, as they stared at her office door.

"He can keep his stinking promises. Hire him and I'll be out of here faster than she was."

"You're punishing him," she whispered. "Don't you think he's suffered, too?"

"Good. I hope to hell he has."

"You don't mean that!"

"Don't I?"

"But what about Bridget?" What about me? her heart cried. What about our love? Are you going to turn your back on me, too?

His eyes remained on the closed door. The only means he had of protecting Jennifer and the whole town from his father was to stand firm. Jebediah Jones would ruin everything; he always had, he always would.

"Bridget broke her date to the prom—thanks to the smut written on the walls. She can stay at Sophie's house or I'll take her with me. She can finish school in Kansas City. We'll both walk.''

Hurt beyond measure that he could cut her from his life with such ease, Jennifer felt her compassion for Jebediah Jones expand. Physically, Duke was a carbon copy of his father; emotionally, he copied his mother's temperament.

''Run,'' she mumbled, slowly rising to her feet. ''Don't you mean run? When do you stop running? When do you stop being afraid you're going to turn out to be just like your father? What's it going to take for you to *care* enough to stick around?''

''I do care,'' Duke refuted. ''You know I care.''

''Do I? I'm the lady with the photographic memory. You once told me you don't ask for what you haven't earned and you don't want for things you don't need for survival. You don't need *me* any more than you need your father!''

''I love you, Jenny. Don't doubt that for a minute.''

''I'm a Missourian. You'll have to show me.'' Her knees wobbled, but she mustered the fortitude she needed to cross to her office door. ''Show me you'll be there when your father needs you. Be at the town meeting tomorrow...with your father at your side.''

''Think, Jenny-love. Don't let your heart rule your head! You made me eat my words. What about what you said? What was your goal before I arrived in Lumberton? To increase employment opportunities here, that's what you wanted most. You can do it! You can read the speech on your desk and convince people to follow your lead. You're a McMann! They'd follow you. No one will follow me! No one will follow my father! Don't throw everything you've worked for away on the Joneses!''

Grieved by his stubbornness, she sadly nodded her head. He'd leave her and his hometown. And he'd feel as though he was doing the right thing. Love wouldn't keep him here. She'd failed him just as surely as his father had failed him.

He'd taught her to read, but she'd failed to teach him how to care.

But, because she cared, because she loved him, she couldn't let him depart without expressing her gratitude for the changes he'd made in all their lives.

"You taught me to read. For that I thank you with all my heart. And I thank you on behalf of the townspeople for breathing life back into this town." She turned the doorknob and backed into her office. "We'll miss you, Duke Jones."

Chapter Fourteen

He's right," Jebediah Jones admitted. "You are better off without hiring me."

"You listened at the door?"

"Yeah, up to the point where he finished talking about my wife. I had to sit down then."

Stepping around the corner of her desk, she mentally replayed what had been said. Jebediah hadn't heard Duke's ultimatum: hire him and I walk. Nor had he heard her acknowledgment of what Duke had done or her thanking him. The private part of their conversation remained inviolate.

"Mostly, what he told you was the truth," Jebediah said as she sat down. "What he doesn't know is how I felt. I didn't think she'd really leave town. And if she did, I convinced myself she wouldn't be gone long."

Underneath her rigid composure Jennifer cringed, knowing he had voiced her hopes. He'd also confirmed her worst fear. As she'd thanked Duke, she'd thought, Duke won't leave; he'll be back.

Pangs of anxiety hammered in her chest. Should she politely excuse herself and run after Duke? What more could she say once she caught up with him? I refused to discuss employment opportunities at the marble quarry with your father? I kicked the drunken bum out of my office? I know what I'm doing isn't right or fair or . . .

Lost in her own private hell, she jumped when Jebediah touched her arm to get her attention.

"I desperately want a job in the marble quarry. Do you know why?"

She mutely shook her head, mentally comparing the difference in the two men's touch. The father's hand was soft, and yet she could feel the same strength she felt when Duke touched her with his callused hands. "Why?"

"To keep the vow I made to Celeste. I told her I'd go back to work if the quarry opened. I mean to keep my word."

He removed his hand from her sleeve and let it fall limply between his knees; he scrutinized it as though it belonged to a stranger. "Oh, yeah, I know what you're thinking. You're too late, old man. There's too many bottles of Kentucky's cheapest whiskey in your belly. Maybe, maybe not." He rubbed his hands on his knee and met her eye to eye. "But let me tell you something, Mayor, I know more about Missouri marble than most experts with fancy degrees. I'd tell you to ask anybody who worked in the quarry, but I know they don't have kind words to say about Jebediah Jones."

His candor had emotional appeal, but she had to rely on more than instincts. She needed solid facts before she could recommend him.

"Sophie Clarmont would remember, wouldn't she?"

A flicker of hope lit his face. "Her father lit the first bundle of dynamite. She's a fair woman. I reckon she could tell you anything her father might've said."

"Can you think of any other person? I need references."

Jebediah thought for a minute, then made a *tsk*ing noise. "I'm afraid you'll hear different versions of my son's opinion.... Wait just a gol-darned minute! There is something. The folks who owned the quarry used to have a company paper. My name was mentioned once or twice."

"Do you have copies of them?"

"Sure do!" His face lit with pride. "Celeste wanted to frame them. I haven't seen hide nor hair of them in years, but I imagine they're packed away in a trunk."

"Good. You find them and bring them here tomorrow."

"Does that mean you might hire me?"

"I have a policy of hiring the best-qualified man available for any job openings."

Jebediah chuckled. With a spryness that defied his age, he jumped to his feet and headed to the door. "Well, ma'am, I figure I've got a good chance. It's good to know the whisper campaign to get you elected is true. You can't read a stop sign, but you go the extra mile to be fair."

She was halfway to her feet when he closed the door. Her knees folded. She landed in her chair with a plop. Her mouth dropped open to utter the same phrase she'd said after hiring Duke. "Oh, my God!"

True to her word, Jennifer left the office and went straight to Sophie's house to get a personal recommendation for Jebediah. At least that was the excuse she gave for arriving on the doorstep where Duke lived. She didn't stop to analyze why she'd packed up the brochures, contracts and leases for Duke's project.

"Come in, dear, I was planning on calling you." Sophie glanced upward at the ceiling as a loud thud made the entry light sway. "Duke paid his room rent and he's packing his belongings."

"We've had a disagreement," Jennifer said. She lowered the box she'd carried to the floor.

"Nothing compared to what happened between Duke and Bridget, I hope." She ushered Jennifer into the parlor. Both women took a seat on the flowered sofa. "I'm surprised you couldn't hear them down at city hall! Sheriff Elmo was almost flattened when Bridget ran through the front door."

"You had to call Big Jim?"

"No, dear, the sheriff came by to see if Duke had buried incriminating evidence in the back shed." Sophie stifled a giggle with her hand. "At noon today, some busybody saw Duke stealthily entering the shed with a shovel and a bag of concrete. When Duke came out polishing what looked like a piece of marble from a tombstone, this person figured I'd met an untimely demise. Murder on Elm Street, Part Two."

Jennifer groaned aloud. "Duke must be livid!"

"He doesn't know why Big Jim was here. If he weren't in such a foul mood, he'd have roared with laughter." Sophie's eyes danced with contained mirth. "I wish I'd gotten a snapshot of the expression on Big Jim's face. Once he discovered that I wasn't the victim, he insisted on inspecting the shed. He muttered something about stolen goods and bank heists."

"You could have stopped him. He didn't have a search warrant, did he?"

"Noooo, sirrreee, bobtail," Sophie drawled, imitating Big Jim's favorite expression. "But who am I to stop a lawman with a drawn pistol in his hand from making a complete fool of himself?" Sophie chuckled. "Big Jim ran from tree to tree until he got to the shed, then he flung the door off its hinges and shouted, 'Police. Stick 'em up.'"

Despite her problems, Jennifer had to laugh.

"Those bathroom sinks peacefully surrendered without a word," Sophie concluded, slapping her ample thigh. "Yes, sirrree, Big Jim wins the Crimestopper of the Week award."

Heavy footsteps coming down the stairs erased the grin on Jennifer's face. Automatically, she rose to her feet.

"We're in the parlor, Duke," Sophie called. She tugged the hem of Jennifer's skirt and whispered, "Can you make him change his mind about leaving here?"

Jennifer was shaking her head when Duke dropped his suitcases in front of the door beside her cardboard box.

"You did it, didn't you?" he demanded, his face contorted in misery.

Jennifer quoted Jebediah. "The mayor can't read a stop sign, but she goes the extra mile to be fair."

His eyes guiltily dropped to Sophie.

Levering herself off the couch, Sophie let her glasses slide to the tip of her nose and gaily announced, "What we all need is a nice cold glass of freshly squeezed lemonade. If you'll excuse me, I'll go into the kitchen and nuke some."

"She's known all along," Jennifer hissed when she heard the kitchen door slam closed. At least somebody in this town respected their privacy! She took a step forward; Duke took one backward. "Do you realize the mental gymnastics I went through to hide the fact that I couldn't read? Taping the mail...carrying around books...eating hamburgers in unfamiliar restaurants..." She folded her arms across her chest to keep from emphasizing each example by rapping him in the middle of his chest with her fist. "You could have told me!"

"Sophie didn't tell me until after you did. And when she did tell me, it wasn't as though she'd revealed a big secret. You should have asked her to help you years ago."

"Ha! And spoil everybody's fun? Why didn't Sophie tell *me*?"

"Because she knew you were ashamed. She hoped that one day you would tell her yourself."

"Pardon me if I don't jump up and down with joy knowing the best-kept secret in Lumberton is about the town's mayor! How should I feel right now?" she asked sarcastically. "Sublimely happy?"

"What was the *fair* thing for me to do?"

"You should have told me!"

"Well, I didn't. So hang me!"

Jennifer marched around him giving him a wide berth. "I'll let you have that pleasure." She kicked the box she'd carried against his suitcase, knocking it flat. "This is your brilliant idea. You've done all the work on it. You scheduled the town meeting on Saturday. You even wrote a speech for me to R-E-A-D! You treated your father like a lame horse ready for the glue factory. Well, Mr. Duke Jones, I don't think it's fair to shoot horses or to hang frogs! You'll get that pleasure."

Never having seen Jennifer be anything other than sweet and kind, Duke was taken aback by her vehement attack. "What do you mean?"

"You aren't going anywhere! You're going to H-A-N-G around until the town meeting because I'm not going to further humiliate myself by reading aloud in public." Her voice raised an octave as she bellowed, "It's your baby! You take care of it!"

A tray of glasses crashed to the floor in the kitchen at the same moment Jennifer gave the box another kick and dashed through the front door.

Duke started after her but stopped dead in his tracks when he heard Sophie shriek, "Jenny is pregnant!" He raised his hands to the ceiling and prayed for divine intervention.

He did an about-face and marched into the kitchen. "For heaven's sake, Sophie, the windows are open. Why don't you pick up the telephone and inform the west end of town?"

Wide-eyed, Sophie pushed her glasses up the bridge of her nose and whispered in a schoolmarmish voice, "I ought to spank your little fanny for this stunt!"

"Jenny is not pregnant!"

She shook her finger in his face. "Don't you lie to me, Duke Jones!"

"She isn't pregnant. She was talking about the vanity project being my baby." Duke dropped to his haunches and began picking up the slivers of glass. "She dumped it in my lap."

"Good for her! I keep telling you how smart she is." Sophie ambled to the broom closet. Broom and dustpan in hand, she brushed Duke aside. "You go after her."

"Much as I hate to admit it, we can't settle our problems over a glass of lemonade, Sophie." He remained on his knees, his head bowed. "There's a man who has shadowed me all his life that is standing between us."

"Jebediah?"

"She's going to hire him to work at the quarry. You know him, Sophie. He's going to ruin everything."

"I know what he is . . . and I know what he used to be. In Jennifer's shoes, I'd give the man a chance." She glared at Duke. "Don't you dare call me Soft Soap Sophie, like Big Jim does, or I'll carry your suitcases out to that meat grinder you call a motorcycle and strap them on myself! That's if your sister doesn't beat me to it."

"She doesn't want to leave." He held the dustpan for her to sweep the shards of glass into. "She patched things up with Chad Felton."

"Admit it, Duke. You aren't going anywhere, either. Like it or not, you're part of this town. Lumberton is sort of like Jennifer's brother. You love it, but you don't always like it."

"It's never liked me," Duke pointed out.

"But you won't stand by and watch Lumberton become a ghost town any more than Jennifer would stand by and let something awful happen to George."

She reached to the counter for a damp cloth, tossed it on the floor, stepped on it and began making circular motions with her foot.

"Let me do that," Duke volunteered.

"Nope. I make a mess; I clean it up. That way no one can fuss at me for making a mistake." She shoved her spectacles into place. "Not a bad motto, Duke. You ought to try it."

"I wouldn't know where to begin."

"Jennifer cared enough to help you get a job. Why don't you start by caring enough to help other people have the same chance she gave you?"

"The town meeting? You think I should stand up at the podium and have rotten eggs thrown at me?"

"Rotten eggs stink a mite, but they'll wash off. Sometimes when you're slapped in the face you have to turn the other cheek."

"I've had both cheeks slapped." Duke grinned ruefully. "That only leaves the bottom two. Are you suggesting I drop my drawers and moon the good citizens of Lumberton?"

"Rascal!" Sophie laughed in spite of herself. "No silver paper stars for that wisecrack, young man."

Duke rose from his knees and started toward the front door.

"Where are you going?" Sophie asked, afraid he'd taken her quip seriously.

"Nowhere."

Jennifer listened as closely to what Sheriff Elmo said as she had listened last night for the sound of a Harley motorcycle laying a strip of rubber down Elm Street. Then, as now, the only thing she heard was Big Jim huffing and puffing.

"He's up to no good, that's for sure," Big Jim railed. "There's something mighty peculiar going on out in that shed." He glanced at Sophie. "I don't suppose you're adding three bathrooms in your back-yard, are you?"

"Why don't you spend the day investigating the construction permits?" Sophie replied. Her eyes twinkled with mischief. "Look under outhouses."

Milly twittered; Tim Farrell blinked sleepily.

Jennifer eyed Sophie suspiciously. For a woman who was usually chatty with her, Sophie had been mysteriously silent when she'd been making coffee and Jennifer had brought up Duke's name. The only thing she'd been able to pry from Sophie's tight lips was a brief message from Duke: be at the town meeting.

"Tomorrow I want Main Street blocked with bar-ricades," she said, looking from Sophie to Big Jim. "I expect we'll be having a big crowd. I understand the maintenance department is setting up the Fourth of July stage?"

Sophie nodded, lips sealed.

"You're mighty damned quiet lately," Big Jim commented, forgetting to excuse himself for his mild expletive.

Sophie covered her eyes, her ears and then her mouth.

The square was jam-packed. Pickup trucks lined the streets. No one Jennifer talked to remembered downtown Lumberton ever being so crowded, not even on Fourth of July.

Jennifer sat up on the stage, flanked on one side by Clementine's father and on the other by Reverend Walters and Milly. She held her speech, which Sophie had delivered to her house this morning, corkscrewed in her hands.

Did Duke actually believe she was going to stand up and stutter her way through the three pages of bold-typed print? If he wanted her to speak, he should have given her time to memorize what he wanted said. The only reason she'd brought it along was for someone else to read.

To keep her growing panic under control, she concentrated on the three marble vanities displayed on the front steps of city hall. Sunlight reflected off the polished surface, attracting the attention of the townspeople strolling by them.

Occasionally she could hear the oohs and aahs and the ''I want one of those in our house'' that the wives were saying.

Where is he? she asked silently. She watched for him, at first furtively and with each passing minute more openly. Her eyes dropped to her lap, where her hands were tightly laced. She separated her fingers and stared at the palm Duke had kissed. He'd told her to save the kiss for a lonely day, but she'd had no idea what loneliness was until Duke had vanished from her life.

Why was it when she was trying so hard to be wise, she ended up doing something completely dumb?

She'd known the relationship between Duke and his father had been strained for years. Why did she think she could heal those wounds by saying, "Give the man the same chance I gave you?" Not too brilliant. She hadn't been wounded by Jebediah the way Duke had been hurt. What did she know of Duke's pain and anguish?

The most stupid thing she'd done was to act as judge and jury on Duke's behavior by waving a banner lettered with one word: Fair. Was it fair that she was mayor of Lumberton? Despite everyone's knowing she was illiterate, she'd inherited the votes that elected her. In the name of fairness, she'd asked the two men who'd applied for jobs for proof of their qualification for the jobs. And yet, when it came to filling the most important job in the city, the mayorship, she'd relied on being a McMann.

She hoped and prayed that by being on this platform, she'd finally be scrupulously fair.

Her stomach growled as it rolled from side to side. She hadn't eaten breakfast, but on the other hand, she figured she'd be eating plenty of crow before the morning was over.

"There he is," she heard someone whisper. "Over there!"

People had crowded around the stage. She had to sit up in her seat and straighten her shoulders to see over their heads.

Her eyes widened in shock.

There, standing in front of George's grocery store, was the high-school marching band. The cheerleaders, with their blue-and-gold pom-poms, waved to the people still loitering in the shops, encouraging them to join the parade.

In front of a row of trombonists were three men: Duke Jones, George McMann and Jebediah Jones.

She jumped to her feet. Out of habit, she touched the small device in her ear when she should have been rubbing her eyes to clear up her hallucination.

"George?" she muttered. "With Duke? Father and son marching side by side?"

Like Reverend Walters, Jennifer checked the clear sky to see if bolts of lightning would drop. Surely the ground had to be trembling beneath her feet.

The trumpets blared; the bass drum pounded; the trombone slides jerked up and down.

Jennifer tugged on Bill's sleeve. "What song are they playing?"

"'Seventy-six Trombones'!"

She grinned for the first time in two days. There was no doubt in her mind as to why Duke had chosen that particular tune. Before he climbed up on the platform, he was showing the townspeople as he marched down the street that he wasn't a shyster. He wouldn't trick them out of their money and abscond from town. He was here to stay and he wanted them to know it.

Duke waved to the crowd, but his eyes searched the platform for Jenny. He'd been scared spitless when Sophie had been at Jennifer's house. What-ifs, combined with his self-doubts, were killing him. He'd damned his temper and his pride. He'd struggled with his conscience, trying to be fair. And while he'd battled his inner wars, he'd worked twenty hours each day preparing for this moment.

It had taken guts to go to George and convince him to back this project. They'd almost come to blows. But George was a businessman who stood to make a substantial profit from starting a factory. People who moved away from town didn't eat. He still owned the only grocery store in town. After Duke settled him down long enough to present the facts and figures, George completely forgot to bully Duke.

Slanting a quick glance in Jebediah's direction, Duke edged closer, ready to wrap his arm around his father's shoulder and steady him if necessary. It took courage for the man who'd been known as the town drunkard to walk down the center line of Main Street. Steady as a rock, Jebediah put one foot in front of the other in perfect beat with the band.

Yesterday, Duke had made a pact with his father. He'd make certain Jebediah would have a chance for the job he wanted, on one condition. His father would continue the search he'd started. Celeste had vowed to return when Jebediah got a job. Together, maybe— with luck—maybe it wasn't too late.

Stranger things have happened recently, Duke thought, his dark eyes honing in on Jennifer.

Who would ever have believed Duke Jones would become the town's benefactor?

Who would ever have believed he would have fallen in love with the town's mayor?

And wonder of wonders, who would ever have believed that for one short month, Duke Jones had been loved in return?

The marching band blew its final chord. The crowd roared its approval, applauding, whistling and cheering as loudly as it could. As deaf to their cheers as he had been to their whispers, Duke barely noticed how the townspeople parted like the Red Sea to let him stride to the platform.

The sound of his leather soles striking the wooden makeshift steps instantly lowered the volume of the people nearest to the platform. As though cued, those in front turned to the people behind them to shush the noise. Soon quiet rippled to the back of the crowd.

Reverend Walters stood and crossed to the microphone to begin the meeting with a morning prayer.

"Let's all bow our heads, please."

Duke took the minister's seat beside Jennifer. His thigh brushed against the folds of her gathered skirt. He watched the tremor run through her hand as she scooped the fabric aside to make room for him. God, don't let me foul up, he prayed as the minister's voice droned in the background. She's so perfect. Give me the strength and wisdom to earn her respect. Help me convince her that I do care! I care for her to the exclusion of all else, more than I care about being ridiculed in public, more than I minded groveling to her brother, more than anything, I love Jennifer McMann.

"We are gathered together today to listen to an idea that could make some big changes in Lumberton," Reverend Walters said in his melodious church voice. "So let's give a big round of applause for the woman who had the foresight to welcome a black sheep back into the flock!"

Jennifer's eyes flew from Duke's profile to the microphone and back again.

Amid rowdy cheers, she leaned close to Duke's ear and whispered, "I can't read this. It's too hard! I'm going to look like a fool!"

Duke's heart went out to her. Maybe he'd asked too much. His solemn black eyes met her panicked blue eyes. "Those are my words, written from my heart, Jenny-love. If you can't say them, then don't."

He watched her nervously roll the speech into a paper tube. He could tell she was mentally collecting herself when her eyelids closed for a moment.

Jennifer said a hasty prayer, then stood gracefully and crossed to the microphone. She forced a sickly smile on her lips as she flattened the curled paper on the podium. A sea of familiar faces swam in front of her eyes before she let them drop to the printed page.

Her prayer went unanswered; her mind went blank. She couldn't tell a *B* from a *P* from a *D*. The only thing she recognized was the sweat from her fingers leaving a damp imprint on the page. Her fingers had been smaller back then in Sophie's class, but her fear was the same: she couldn't read a word. She was standing in front of the whole damned town and the symbols were meaningless!

Her chin dropped to her waist. "I can't read this," she whispered into the loudspeaker system.

Chapter Fifteen

Read it by heart,'' Sophie shouted, pushing her way through to the front row. The small box clutched in her hand threatened to be knocked to the ground, but she held on to it tenaciously. "Just like you did in my class!"

Jennifer knew what Sophie meant: fake it.

She shook her head. She couldn't fake it any longer.

Her hand visibly shook, but she took the microphone in her hand and clearly, loudly, said, "I can't read this. I can only read on the second-grade level, but I'm working on it."

She expected to hear gasps and hushed whispers; she expected to see heads shaking from side to side in disgust. What she didn't expect was for George to step forward and drape his arm across her shoulder.

"Do we care whether or not the mayor reads Shakespeare?" he asked the crowd.

"No!"

"Do you care about my sister?"

"Yes!" the crowd blared.

"Then let her do what she's always done—tell it from her heart!" While the townspeople clamored their approval, George leaned down to her and whispered in the ear with the hearing device, "I never called you a dumb blonde, sis. You show 'em what kind of stuff a McMann is made of."

Jennifer rapidly blinked; her throat filled with emotion. She glanced over her shoulder at Duke for the encouragement she needed to get through the next few minutes.

He didn't disappoint her. Those black eyes of his burned with his fierce pride in her. She knew as far as he was concerned she was perfect, she could do no wrong. He'd put her up on a pedestal and that was where she remained.

She turned her face back to her friends and neighbors.

"My father had a dream. He dreamed of Lumberton being what it had been when he was a boy. A place where everyone prospered, where everyone could lead a good life, where the young people could grow and thrive and the old people could watch, knowing their grandchildren would have the same opportunities they had."

Her voice started out weak but grew stronger with every phrase.

"I think my dad would be proud if he were here today. With everyone's help, his dream will become reality." She turned, slowly extending her hand toward Duke. "I can't take credit for fulfilling my father's dreams. Only one man can...Duke Jones. I hope you'll all give him a big welcoming hand. He's earned it."

At first, while Duke remained seated, mustering his courage together, there was dead silence.

A sprinkling of hands began to enthusiastically clap: Sophie's, Bridget's, George's.

Duke felt physically ill, wild with fear. Of course they'd all joined in the parade. Who could resist a marching band and cheerleaders? And they couldn't resist applauding their favorite heroine. But they could easily resist welcoming him with open arms.

Move! he silently ordered his limbs. The seat of his pants seemed glued to his folding chair. This is your last chance! Grab it!

Jennifer's hand was his lifeline. He could hear his elbow creak as he reached for it. In slow motion, he rose to his feet, straightening his shoulders.

"Let's hear it for Duke!" he heard his sister shout. She bounded up the steps and cartwheeled across the platform. "Hip, hip..."

"Hooray!" the crowd shouted.

"Hip, hip..."

"Hooray!"

"He can't hear you! One more time! HIP! HIP!"

"HOORAY!" the crowd thundered, hands clapping, feet stomping.

Bridget executed a perfect forward flip off the platform. Smiling, Jennifer took Duke's hand.

Big Jim Elmo roared over the cheers, "You've all lost you're ever-lovin' minds! That ring-tailed polecat is gonna—" But his protest was drowned in another chorus of cheers as Jennifer raised her hand, linked to Duke's, high in the air. Realizing those people stomping and clapping were the same people who'd elected him to office, Big Jim grimaced and began to applaud.

Caught up in the fervor, Milly Walters jumped to her feet and yelled, "Give 'em hell, Duke!" Realizing who she was and what she'd said in front of God and everybody, she clamped her hands over her mouth.

"Sit down, Milly," her husband said softly. "I reckon Duke doesn't need any encouragement of that nature."

Jennifer joined her fingers with Duke's and raised their hands high in the air.

Several minutes passed before the noise died down enough for Duke to be heard. Jennifer tried to take her seat back behind Duke, but he shook his head as she tried to tug her fingers from his.

"My dreams were nightmares," he began, his voice husky with raw sentiment. "Like a scared kid, I ran and ran through a pitch-black tunnel, searching for a guiding light. You can imagine how surprised I was when I opened my eyes and found myself right back where I'd started. Thanks to Jenny, I've realized the light would never come from an outside source. It shines brightly from within our souls."

His eyes illuminated with hope.

"What I'm proposing to end each of your private nightmares is going to take work. Hard work. Pulling together instead of pulling apart." He searched the crowd, looking for Phil and Bertha as he plucked the plans he'd written on several sheets of paper from the inside pocket of his sports jacket. "You're going to have to set aside your private feuds. You'll have bigger things to worry about than leash laws and hauling your trash to the curbs."

He leaned across the speaker's stand toward Clementine and her father. "If you two will start passing out those stacks of paper, we'll start working together, right now. Jenny fed the grapevine when she called many of you on the telephone. I think it's time to harvest the crop. The first page is a shareholder's agreement the company's lawyer drew up. Everyone is eligible. We hope you'll all take part. How much is not important."

"On page two, you'll find..."

Absorbed in building the foundation for the ABC Marble Fixture Company, Duke let go of Jennifer's hand to turn the pages. She stood there, her eyes roaming the circle that had formed a tight knot and was moving closer and closer to the speaker's podium.

The leaders of the community stood shoulder to shoulder with the farmers, avidly listening as Duke listed the names of the people who'd volunteered to form a committee for each department of the company.

It was difficult to believe these were the same people who'd labeled the Jones family as poor white trash. These were the people Duke had tried to impress, whose approval he'd desperately needed. He's reached his goal, Jennifer mused, slowly backing away from Duke until the backs of her knees touched her empty chair. She dropped into it, picked up her purse from off the rough-hewed timbers and removed a notepad and pen.

No one noticed her painstakingly write three words on a sheet of paper, fold it and put it on the seat of her chair, then silently slip off the back of the stage.

Too restless to sit through the business portion of the meeting without being a disruption, she fled. She was at the corner of Main and Elm streets when she stopped running and paused to catch her breath.

"He did it!" she crowed, dancing an impromptu jig and hugging herself. She was so proud of him she thought she'd burst with happiness. He didn't need a McMann standing beside him or supporting him from behind. "He's his own man."

My man! her heart silently sang.

Duke felt certain he'd shaken the hand of every man, woman and child in Lumberton. The muscles in his face ached from smiling; his knuckles were sore from having them squeezed; his arm felt like a rusty water pump. He'd locked his knees for such a long period of time the muscles in his calves threatened to knot into Charley horses.

And all the while, the note he'd picked up off Jenny's chair burned a hole through his shirt to his heart.

He knew better than to doubt her.

Yes, he knew better, but that didn't stop him from wondering if he'd inadvertently done something to offend her.

"'Scuse me, please. 'Scuse me." Sophie had waited until the crowd had thinned around Duke to congratulate him on a job well done. "Oh, Duke, could I speak to you for just a moment? Privately?"

"Would you excuse me?" Duke said to the Feltons. Grinning, he added, "My first-grade teacher is calling me."

Sophie and Duke walked rapidly away from the others.

"I've got something for you. I doubt you'll remember, but I always rewarded my children when they did something especially well." They stopped near the corner of the square under a pin oak tree. She placed the small, flat box in his hand. "I won't embarrass you by pasting them on your forehead."

He lifted the lid knowing what he'd find inside. "Paper stars."

"Gold stars—they're harder to come by than silver stars."

Grinning, he put the lid back on them, then wrapped his arms around Sophie and swung her plump body right off her feet.

Giggling like a schoolgirl, Sophie squealed, "Put me down!"

"Uh-uh. I'm paying you back for all those hugs you gave me when I was a kid."

"Enough! Let go of me and go find the woman who deserves your hugs!"

Restoring Sophie's feet to the ground, he held on to her until she'd recovered her balance, then reached into his pocket and pulled out Jennifer's note.

What he read made his heart swell. There was a spelling error in the key word, but the meaning was more important than the rule about the silent *e* at the end of a word.

* * *

Jennifer stooped, picking up the most perfectly flat, rounded rock she'd ever found beside the lake. She rubbed her thumb over the weathered limestone.

"Five, maybe six jumps," she calculated. Puffed up with the exuberance of having ridden her dirt bike over the trail at a record-breaking pace, she changed her mind. "Eight."

"Do I hear you counting backward? Starting without me?"

Laughing, Jennifer pivoted around on one foot and watched him skid down his steep shortcut path. "Be careful! You're ruining your new clothes!"

"Who cares?"

She was in his arms, peppering his beloved face with kisses, before she answered, "You care."

"I'm a slow learner. It took me longer than it took you to learn how to read, but, yeah, I do care."

"You're wonderful," she crooned, rewarding him with a prolonged kiss, a robust kiss that mellowed to one filled with passion. "You're so wonderful."

His hand slid up to cover her heart. She'd changed from her dress into pale blue shorts and a rough-woven top, and from the moment he'd seen her his fingers had longed to touch its rough texture before he touched her satin smooth skin. Her heart pounded, hard and heavy.

"Keep telling me that for the next million years and maybe I'll begin to believe it."

"You'll be around that long?" she whispered, needing to hear him tell her again that he'd be around for as long as she wanted him.

"Longer than those limestone cliffs," he promised. "Even when I packed my bags, I knew I couldn't leave. Not unless you went with me. I knew you weren't going anywhere."

"Oh, but I would have. I can read a map and road signs. I'd have followed you anywhere you went."

He unsnapped the front latch of her bra. "I don't want to be anywhere else but here, with you." His dark head dipped to take love bites of her firm flesh. "Jenny-love, will you marry me?" His mouth closed hotly around her nipple.

"How could I refuse? You've found the nicest way of persuading me."

She helped him shrug out of his jacket and shirt; he helped her remove her top and shorts. Tiny kisses, sharp groans of passion and words of love punctuated the string of buttons, snaps and zippers being undone.

They spread the tangle of clothing on a smooth place Duke cleared of pebbles with his hands.

When she'd stretched out, Duke dropped beside her, capturing her face between his hands. Though glazed with desire, his eyes sparkled with mirth. "I want you to be fully aware of what will happen if you do marry me."

"I'll marry you. Don't talk to me of consequences, just show me how much you love me." Her skin felt hotter than the sun shining overhead. Agitated by frustration, her hands skittered across his forearms to his shoulders. "Show me!"

He raised himself over her, kneeling between her thighs, letting his furred chest move against the moisture on her breasts, still damp from his mouth's caresses. Friction created by his body rubbing against her lit the fires of passion. The warm tingling sensation of desire spread over her, licking her more thoroughly than Duke's ravishing tongue.

"I love you, Jenny-love. Spell it with or without an *e* and when I read it I'll feel like weeping for joy." He rocked back on his haunches and placed his lips low on her stomach. "I want to be the father of your children."

"Oh, yes, please," she sighed, sucking in her stomach until it was concave. "Give me your baby, Duke."

His lips drifted over the cluster of honey-blond curls. With his hands on her breasts, he lowered his head farther and kissed her as she'd never been kissed.

She wove her hands through his dark hair and tugged upward. "No, Duke."

"Don't be afraid, Jenny." With the taste of her on his lips, he wanted to finish what he'd begun. "Let me love you completely. Loving each other, there's nothing you and I can do to cause shame."

"You don't understand, love." Her knees clenched against his shoulders. Caught in the upward spiraling passions caused by his lips and tongue, she feared she'd reach the pinnacle without him. "I need you too much. Now. Come home to me."

He put an end to her torment by possessing her with the fierce passion of a man who'd do anything for her. His hips rose and fell rhythmically as he plunged deep within her womanly softness. She closed tightly about him.

They gave and took pleasure equally in a heated, intensely satisfying physical exchange of love.

When they had climbed to the highest peak, they shared it. He spilled his seed deeply inside of her with both of them hoping—no, praying—that it would find fertile ground.

It was a short while later, as they dried each other after a dip in the lake, that Duke said, "Marry me and you'll be Mayor Jones. Does that bother you?"

Playfully, Jennifer popped his bare bottom with her shirt.

"You'll be the mother of the Jones kids," he warned, grinning, loving the idea.

"You're going to keep me barefoot and pregnant? At city hall?" She shook her silver blond hair as she reclined on the flat rock beside the lake. "I don't think those two go together."

"I won't let you resign."

Jennifer chuckled, rubbing her hand over her stomach. Her eyes drifted closed as a new daydream began forming in her mind.

"With luck, I'll finish my term of office about the same time the baby arrives...and you get elected mayor."

"Me?" Astounded, he almost dropped the tiny box he'd removed from his jacket pocket. He stretched out beside her, then opened the box of golden paper stars. "Mayor of Lumberton?"

"Why not?" She smiled as she felt a moist kiss planted in the center of her forehead. "You'd do a good job."

Contented with his not arguing the point with her, the daydream swelled, unfurling all sorts of possibilities. She had always done her best creative thinking here at the lake.

"I love this place," she whispered. "Almost as much as I love you."

"L-O-V?"

She heard the faint rustling of paper. "Love, what are you doing?"

"Making certain everyone knows you're perfect."

He pasted another star on her forehead, smiling, knowing she'd remove them before they got back to town.

Jennifer groaned and lazily opened one eye. "You aren't preparing something for me to read, are you?"

"Nope." He put a damp fingertip in the box of stars. Small, golden stars clung to his fingertip. "Repeat after me.... There was a little girl who had a little star, right in the middle of her forehead. And when she was good, she was very, very good..."

"I know that nursery rhyme! And when she was bad she was—"

"Very, very good," he finished, kissing her. "Very, very good."

* * * * *

NORA ROBERTS
brings you the first
Award of Excellence title
Gabriel's Angel
coming in August from
Silhouette Intimate Moments

They were on a collision course with love....

Laura Malone was alone, scared—and pregnant. She was running for the sake of her child. Gabriel Bradley had his own problems. He had neither the need nor the inclination to get involved in someone else's.

But Laura was like no other woman... and she needed him. Soon Gabe was willing to risk all for the heaven of her arms.

The Award of Excellence is given to one specially selected title per month. Look for the second Award of Excellence title, coming out in September from Silhouette Romance—**SUTTON'S WAY**
by Diana Palmer

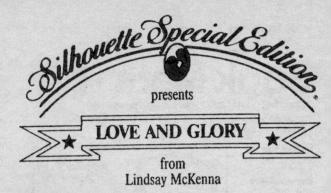

Silhouette Special Edition

presents

LOVE AND GLORY

from
Lindsay McKenna

Introducing a gripping new series celebrating our men—and women—in uniform. Meet the Trayherns, a military family as proud and colorful as the American flag, a family fighting the shadow of dishonor, a family determined to triumph—with **LOVE AND GLORY!**

June: A QUESTION OF HONOR (SE #529) leads the fast-paced excitement. When Coast Guard officer Noah Trayhern offers Kit Anderson a safe house, he unwittingly endangers his own guarded emotions.

July: NO SURRENDER (SE #535) Navy pilot Alyssa Trayhern's assignment with arrogant jet jockey Clay Cantrell threatens her career—and her heart—with a crash landing!

August: RETURN OF A HERO (SE #541) Strike up the band to welcome home a man whose top-secret reappearance will make headline news . . . with a delicate, daring woman by his side.
